The Dom's Submission

His Submission

Book 3

Ellis O. Day

I love to hear from readers so email me at
authorellisoday@gmail.com

https://www.EllisODay.com

Facebook
https://www.facebook.com/EllisODayRomanceAuthor/

Closed FB Group (sneak peeks, sample chapters, and other bonuses)
https://www.facebook.com/groups/153238782143373

Twitter
https://twitter.com/ellis_o_day

Pinterest
www.pinterest.com\AuthorEllisODay

Other Books By Ellis O. Day:

GO TO MY WEBSITE TO SEE ALL MY BOOKS AND TO SEE WHAT'S COMING NEXT
HTTPS://WWW.ELLISODAY.COM

SIX NIGHTS OF SIN SERIES (BOOKS 1-6)
(AVAILABLE IN PAPERBACK AND EBOOK)

SIX NIGHTS OF SIN SERIES EBOOK ONLY
INTERVIEWING FOR HER LOVER (BOOK 1)
EBOOK IS FREE
TAKING CONTROL (BOOK 2)
SCHOOL FANTASY (BOOK 3)
MASTER – SLAVE FANTASY (BOOK 4)
PUNISHMENT FANTASY (BOOK 5)
THE PROPOSITION (BOOK 6)

THE VOYEUR SERIES (BOOKS 1-4)
(AVAILABLE IN PAPERBACK AND EBOOK)

THE VOYEUR SERIES EBOOK ONLY
The Voyeur (Book One) **FREE**
Watching the Voyeur (Book Two)
Touching the Voyeur (Book Three)
Loving the Voyeur (Book Four)

A Merry Masquerade For Christmas

(AVAILABLE IN PAPERBACK AND EBOOK)

CHAPTER 1: Terry

Terry sat in the business part of the Club, not in the office with Ethan. It was Saturday night, over twenty-four hours since the fight, and Maggie still hadn't called him. They were done. Finished. He tossed back another drink.

"Hey, Ethan said you were in here." Nick sat next to him at the bar.

"Yep." He waved his hand and the bartender filled his glass. "Glenlivet for him too." He nodded at Nick.

"Thanks," said Nick as the bartender returned with his drink.

"What are you doing here?" asked Terry. "Finally see the light and realize men weren't created to be monogamous."

"No, nothing like that." Nick smiled. "Sarah's out with her sister and Annie."

"Does that mean Patrick's coming here too?" He took a gulp of his drink. "That's cause for celebration."

"No. Patrick is upstairs with Ethan. We're getting ready for poker. You should join us."

"Later. First, you guys should come down and we can find us some women. Just like the old days."

"Not interested."

"You make me embarrassed to be a man." His eyes roamed the Club. "There are a ton of beautiful, eager, horny women and you want to hide upstairs and play poker."

"Ethan said you and Maggie had another fight. Come upstairs and talk to us. Maybe, we can help."

"I don't need your fucking help." He tossed back his drink. "I need to get laid." His eyes landed on Desiree, one of Ethan's newer employees. "By her."

The bartender filled his drink.

"Don't do this."

He tipped his glass in the young woman's direction. "She's exquisite."

Nick's eyes roamed over her. "She is, but she's not worth it."

He knew what Nick meant but decided to play dumb. "I have more money than I can spend. She's worth whatever price she wants."

"That's not what I meant and you know it." Nick turned to him. "Don't throw away what you have with Maggie over one stupid fight."

"I'm not." His chest tightened and his stomach twisted, adding another knot to his tangled mess of emotions. "It's over between us."

"Only if you want it to be or if you do this."

"You don't know shit." He gulped down the drink and ordered another. "I thought she was special but she's not going to work."

"Just because she won't take your money? That's the stupidest thing I've ever heard. You, of all people, should appreciate that about her."

"I don't give a damn about the money."

"Then what is it?"

"She doesn't trust me."

"Are you sure? I thought that about Sarah too and she did trust me. She just had to deal with some issues of her own."

"I'm sure." He was done with this conversation. It was bringing him down and he'd spent a fortune and many hours drinking his way to happy. "And, I'm sure that I'm going to fuck that exotic, young woman over there."

"Terry, come upstairs. Don't make this decision when you're drunk."

That was the only time he could because when he was sober, he only wanted Maggie. "Nope. I need pussy." He stood.

Nick grabbed his arm. "And you can have it, later. Sober up first." He looked at Ethan's new hire. "She'll appreciate you more if you're not sloppy drunk when you fuck her."

"I'm not a novice. I know how to please a woman drunk or sober." He jerked free and staggered a bit, grabbing onto a chair to steady himself. "Go. Play poker. I've got plans."

He made his way across the bar. The young woman watched him, a hint of a smile on her full, gorgeous lips.

He stopped by her side. "May I buy you a drink?"

"Absolutely." She smiled at him.

"You're stunning." He plopped down next to her, waving the bartender over.

"Thank you." She turned toward the bartender. "Soda water with lime."

"Not drinking?" He couldn't take his eyes from her. She was the most beautiful woman he'd ever seen with jet-black hair, pale complexion and blue eyes. She could be Irish but the tip to her eyes spoke of something else in her blood.

"I've already had two and I don't like to get drunk."

"Really?" Most of the women here drank quite a bit.

Actually, so did the men.

"I find a little is better." She took a sip and his eyes locked on her luscious, red lips.

"Fuck, you're beautiful."

"Thank you." She smiled at him again. "You're not so bad yourself."

"Let's go to a room."

"Wow. You move fast."

"You should be used to that." He caressed the bracelet she wore, telling everyone that she was an employee.

"I expect it from some, but I didn't from you." She studied him.

He was surprised by the intelligence in her gaze. Most beautiful women who worked here weren't stupid, but they weren't this smart either. "Why is that?"

"I've been watching you and you didn't seem interested in anything but your drink until your friend arrived."

"I was taking my time." His fingers trailed along the skin of her arm. It was soft and firm but not as soft as Maggie. He pushed the thought away. "Deciding who I wanted to spend my *time* with tonight." And his money.

"I'm honored."

"But are you accepting?" He was pretty sure she was being sarcastic but not positive. Maybe, he shouldn't have drank so much but fuck, he'd needed it to forget Maggie. He leaned down so his breath caressed her ear. "I'll make it well worth your time."

"Hmm. I don't usually go anywhere, let alone to a private room, with a man I've just met."

"You work here." That was exactly what Ethan's employees

did.

She laughed. It was a tinkling, melodious sound that went straight to his balls and caused his dick, which had been sleeping, to wake up.

"I do but that doesn't mean I have to accompany everyone who asks...or anyone who asks. Ethan made that very clear."

"I understand that, but I never met anyone who turned down a handful of cash." Except Maggie. It was just his luck to pick the one woman here who also wasn't interested in his money. Someone must've put a curse on him.

"Now, you have." She held out her hand. "Desiree."

"Terry." He shook her hand and ordered another drink. He'd put up with enough of Maggie's crap he wasn't about to do it with this young woman. "So, Desiree, this is how it's going to work." He stared at her. "I'm going to finish this drink and by the time I'm done, you're either going to agree to go into a private room with me or I'm going to walk away and find someone who isn't so particular." He held up his glass. "Understand?"

"Absolutely." She smiled and clinked her glass against his. "May I ask you some questions to help me decide?"

"Sure." He couldn't blame her. She'd want to know what he wanted but right now he wasn't sure. Part of him wanted to fuck someone, anyone, to make him forget Maggie, but another part wanted to tie someone up and take out his frustrations on her. That settled it. Punishing someone when angry was never a good idea. "I'm a dom but I don't want anything rough, not tonight."

"Why is that?" She seemed genuinely interested.

A few people milled about nearby. "Can we go to the back?

5

Same rules. I finish my drink and you decide to stay or go." He looked around. "Too many ears around here."

Her blue eyes sharpened as she studied him.

"I swear. I won't touch you, unless you agree to stay."

"Okay."

He stood. "At least someone trusts me," he muttered under his breath as he offered her his hand.

"Excuse me?" She put her hand in his.

"Nothing." He led her across the room, his other hand on the small of her back. She was short and curvaceous but thinner than Maggie. Her ass wouldn't be as soft. It wouldn't cradle his dick as well. He took another gulp of his drink. He needed to get Maggie out of his fucking head.

CHAPTER 2: Maggie

Maggie stared at the computer, wanting to cry. Her credit cards were paid off, thanks to the money that Terry had given her to watch the house. She should've known getting paid to live in her own home was too good to be true, especially when she was sent the first three month's payments up front.

She dropped her head in her hands. She had no idea what she was going to do. She needed to earn more than she did as a hostess. The money from the sale of her house, which she still considered hers, wasn't going to last long. She had to find an apartment. That meant she needed first and last month's rent, plus deposit and a deposit on utilities. She inhaled deeply, trying to calm her fears. She could handle this. She'd figure something out.

Stay here and keep taking his money. It makes him happy. It makes you happy. She shoved that thought away. It wouldn't make either of them happy in the long run. Plus, it was wrong. She was not sleeping with a man to keep the roof over her head and food on the table. *Why? She'd done it for years with David.*

That was different. They were married. A team. This thing with Terry was a fling, just sex.

She went into the kitchen and pulled out one of the bottles of wine that Terry had brought over. She opened it and poured a hefty amount in a glass. She went back into the living room and sat down, staring at the computer again, hoping some money would magically appear or a great apartment would pop up for cheap—really, really cheap—but nothing magical happened. This wasn't a fairy tale.

She smiled and took another sip. If it were, her prince charming wouldn't be a sexy, foul-mouthed dom who liked to do wicked things to her. Her nipples hardened at the memories and a persistent throb beat between her legs. She could be tied to his bed right now.

She took another sip of the wine. On an empty stomach, it was making her feel good fast. Perhaps, she should call Terry and accept that she was going to have sex with him for money. She liked money. She liked having sex with him. She could work off what she owed him. Her mind spun trying to imagine what he'd want her to do to pay back that much money. Whatever it was, she was sure she'd enjoy it.

Her phone beeped and she grabbed it. It was a text from her kids, saying goodnight. She texted them back feeling like the worst mother in the world for being disappointed that it wasn't Terry. She stared at the phone. He'd said to call when she was ready to apologize. She wasn't but she could ask him to come over to talk. They'd end up doing a lot more than that, unless it really was over. He'd always called or stopped by after their other fights. Perhaps, he was done with her. She gulped down more wine. She didn't want it to end. Not now. Maybe, never, but that wouldn't happen. It'd end sooner or later and she'd be back in the same situation—no money and no way to earn it.

Still, it didn't have to end right now. It wasn't fair. She hadn't known that the last time they'd been together was it. She'd ask him for one more night. Her stomach twisted. He might say no. She put the phone down. She couldn't take the rejection.

She looked back at the computer but all she saw was Terry. His eyes dark with desire. His face hard with passion. His head between her legs, that dark hair an erotic contrast to her pale thighs. Those broad shoulders spreading her legs. She grabbed her phone. Rejection would be bad, but he might say yes.

CHAPTER 3: Terry

Terry held the door and Desiree sauntered past him into the room. She had a nice ass but not as nice as Maggie's. He gritted his teeth and followed her inside, closing the door behind him.

"Drink?" He walked to the bar.

"I take it, I get a little longer to decide?" She stared at his almost empty glass.

"Same. Until I finish my drink." He grinned. "I may refill it as often as I like though."

She laughed. "I'll have a vodka rocks with lime, please."

He nodded and poured the two drinks. He walked to a chair near the couch where she was sitting and handed her the glass. He sat, taking a sip of his own drink.

"So, back to my question." She was relaxed on the couch in a pose that highlighted all her assets and she had a lot of them.

Her breasts were large and the shirt accentuated them well, showing a hint of cleavage and a little more when she bent forward. She was good at dressing for this job.

"What question was that?" He couldn't remember. He barely remembered the trip to this room.

"Why nothing rough tonight?"

"How old are you?" She was so young, her body untarnished by age.

"Old enough." She smiled. "You know Ethan wouldn't hire anyone even close to eighteen."

"What are you twenty-three?" That was the same age as his daughter.

"Twenty-five."

"Hmm." It was still so young.

"So, why nothing rough *tonight*?"

"Because I'm not in a very good mood." That was the understatement of the century.

"So?"

"Never." He leaned forward. "Ever. Go with a man for kinky sex when he's pissed."

"That's good advice." Her eyes sparkled.

"It is." He leaned back. "And stay away from any dom who wants to play when he's angry." He let his eyes wander down her body.

"Why?" She took a sip of her drink, her tongue peeking out to clean her lips.

His dick pressed against his zipper. "Because a dom should always be in control of the scene and if he's mad, he won't be."

"And why are you so upset *tonight*?" Again, she emphasized the word.

"A woman. Why else?" He frowned, staring into his drink. "You women prance around, shaking your asses and offering us heaven before slamming the door in our faces." He hated women right now. His ex. Maggie. All of them.

"Ah. Unrequited love."

"Not love."

"Really? You didn't seem like the type to get upset over just anyone."

"I'm not but that doesn't mean it's love."

"You care for her though." She stood. "I'll refresh our drinks." She came back a moment later and bent to fill his glass, giving him an eyeful of her breasts.

They were firm and round and perfect. His hands itched to touch them. "Thanks." He took a large gulp of his drink.

"What happened?" She put the bottle on the table and sat back down, taking a sip of her drink.

"With what?" His eyes locked on her red lips.

"With you and this woman you care for."

"Doesn't matter. It's over."

"Seems to matter to you."

"I've drank enough. Are you staying so I can fuck you or not?" He hoped she'd stay because he didn't have the energy to go and find another woman.

"Haven't decided yet."

"Decide soon."

"I will." She scooted forward and he got another peek at her tits. "But I want to know more about you?"

"Ask and I'll answer, but only if you promise to wrap those lips around my cock."

She grinned. Her mouth was wide and lush, perfect for sucking dick. "I think that can be arranged, but you have to answer my questions first."

"Agreed." Good, he didn't have to find someone else.

"What happened with this woman?" She lowered her eyes. "I don't want to make the same mistake."

He burst out laughing. "Oh, don't worry. You won't."

She watched him expectantly.

He didn't have to tell her anything but why not? "She agreed to be my sub but won't let me take care of her. She doesn't trust me enough." Fuck, just saying it was like a hammer to his chest.

"Have you known her long? Sometimes it takes time."

"Long enough." Okay, so it hadn't been that long but she should trust him by now.

"Maybe for you, but you're not the one vulnerable." Her eyes narrowed a bit. "Or are you?"

"No, I'm not." He had nothing at stake, nothing important to lose.

"You should give her more time."

"Not worried about the competition?" She should be because if he had Maggie, Desiree wouldn't be getting his money.

"No." She leaned back, letting her thighs drift open a bit. "A man like you knows what he wants. The rest of us are temporary substitutions."

He couldn't argue with that. "But I can make you wealthy substitutes."

"This isn't just about money."

He hadn't expected that from her. "There's another way that you and Maggie differ. To her, no matter what else we had"—and they'd had a lot—"it was all about the money."

"Oh, she's one of those."

"No. The opposite." He wouldn't be here and miserable if

she'd only wanted his money. "She refuses to take any of my money, even for necessities."

Desiree's eyes widened. "That one I haven't heard before."

"Exactly." He drank some more and sighed. "It'd be perfect it she'd let me take care of her."

"She must really care for you."

"Why would you say that?"

"She won't take your money. There must be some reason."

"There is but it's not caring for me." He took a sip but she waited for him to continue. "She doesn't want to see herself as a whore."

"Oh." Her lips tipped up at the corners, as if she were holding back a smile.

"No offense."

"None taken." She took a drink of her vodka. "It's not an easy thing to accept."

"She wouldn't be a whore."

"Really? What is she doing for your money besides having sex with you?"

"It's more than sex."

"So, you're in a relationship?"

"An arrangement."

"Hmm. I can see why she's confused."

"Enough." He was done talking. "I answered your questions."

"You did."

"Are you going to stay or go?"

"I thought that was already settled."

He waved his hand. "Still, your choice." He leaned back, stretching out his legs. "If you're staying get over here and on your knees. If not, close the door behind you."

"Oh, I'm staying." She stood and walked toward him, unbuttoning her blouse.

She was so fucking hot and young. Too young. Too young for him. "Stop."

She stopped, her hand on a button.

"I can't. We can't."

Her eyes dropped to his pants where there was no bulge. "I can help."

"No." He sat up, leaning forward. "Just go." He pulled his wallet from his pants and held out a wad of bills.

"Alcohol can—"

He put the money on the table. "It's not that." He glared at his glass. "It's never affected me like that"—he glared at his dick—"before."

"And I'm sure it isn't now. Not anything we can't fix." She moved another step closer and got on her knees, her hands skimming up his thighs. "Let me help you."

"No. Stop." He grabbed her wrists. "You're too young. You should be home or in school or raising kids or hanging out in clubs."

"I am doing the last one." She grinned.

"Not this kind of club." He dropped her wrists and flopped back in his chair. "You're my daughter's age."

"But I'm not your daughter."

"I know, but..." The truth was he wanted Maggie. She'd ruined him for anyone else.

Desiree stood and held out her hand.

"What?"

"Come. You're tired. Let me help you sleep."

"No sex." He took her hand.

"Don't worry. I won't take advantage of you." She smiled as she led him into the other room. "Now, take off your shoes and get in bed."

"I'm the dom."

"Okay. Please, Master, take off your shoes and get into bed."

"That's better." He kicked off his shoes and flopped onto the mattress.

"Roll over."

He shot her a glare. "Why?"

"I'm going to massage your back."

"Oh. In that case." He shifted so he was on his stomach and she climbed on top of him, straddling his hips. He was going to punish Maggie big time for this. He should be on his back thrusting inside this hot, young woman instead of lying here with a limp dick like some old eunuch.

Her hands skimmed up his back and over his shoulders, the touch light but getting firmer. "You should go see this woman."

"I don't want to." He said against the pillow.

"Your brain may not, but other parts of you definitely do."

"That's not why. You're too young."

"Please." Her fingers dug into his shoulders and he groaned. "Stop lying to yourself."

"I don't lie. I'm brutally honest." Except about this.

"You don't have to admit anything to me, but you need to be honest with yourself or you may never have sex again."

"Don't ever say that." He slapped at her leg and she laughed.

"Talk to this woman." She continued to work the muscles

16

in his back. "It's not easy to be vulnerable. To admit to needing someone. Not for women or men." Those words were a soft breath in his ear before she kissed his cheek and he drifted off to sleep.

CHAPTER 4: Terry

When Terry woke it took him a minute to realize where the hell he was. He sat up, running his hand down his face as he crawled out of bed. He pulled his wallet from his pocket to double check. Ethan would fire anyone who stole from a client but it had happened.

His credit cards were still there and some money, but not much. He glanced at the table. The cash was gone. He had no idea how much he'd given Desiree, but he'd leave more for her downstairs. She deserved a small fortune for listening to his shit last night.

He grimaced as his gaze landed on the bottle of scotch. If he were younger and more naïve, he'd swear he'd never drink again but that wasn't going to happen. Although, it would be a while. He stumbled to the bathroom and turned on the shower and then turned it off. He had to get home. He'd forgotten about Beast.

He was halfway home when his phone beeped. There was a message from Ethan and a message from Maggie. How the hell had he missed that?

MAGGIE: Can you come over?

"Fuck." He could've been with her instead of limp-dicked and drunk. He stepped on the gas. Her kids wouldn't be home until this afternoon. They had time, plenty of time.

He slowed down as he pulled into his neighborhood. Even though he wanted to get home, shower and go see Maggie, there were too many children around to speed down these streets. He turned the corner, his eyes drifting over a little girl. She looked a lot like Maggie's daughter. His foot slammed on the brake as Maggie's ex came out of the house, carrying the baby and ushering his other son along.

A woman followed him. It was Stephanie Templar. She stared at his car.

He'd been caught gawking. He put it in park and stepped out of his car. "Stephanie?"

"Terry?" She smiled and headed toward him. The man trailing after her. "I haven't seen you in ages."

"I've been busy." His eyes drifted to the guy. It was Maggie's ex. He'd seen the man through the window when David had picked up the kids. "Looks like you have been too."

"David. David Givens." Maggie's ex shifted the baby to his other arm and held out his hand.

Terry wanted to punch the guy in the face. They lived here and Maggie and this man's kids had to move to Southshore. He steadied his nerves and shook the man's hand.

"You live around here?" asked David.

"Down the street." *Where I banged your ex-wife and*

showed her what it was like having a real man between her legs.

"Terry used to come to the homeowner's meetings but he's been absent for months." Stephanie laughed. "I thought you moved."

Only far enough to avoid her obvious attempts at flirtation. "Nope. Just very busy."

"Terry's a lawyer."

"Oh. Nice. I own my own investment company," said David.

"My husband's very successful." She clung to David's arm. "Give him a card."

David nodded and pulled a card from his pocket, offering it to Terry. "You should give me a call."

"Thanks." He accepted the card. "I'll be in touch." He'd definitely be looking into this guy. "I have to run but it was nice seeing you, Stephanie and nice meeting you, David." He strode back to his car.

His mind spun as he drove down the street. Stephanie might have been lying about David's success, but she wasn't a fool. She wouldn't tie herself to a man with no money. She was rich, richer than rich, but she understood that money married money. That meant, something wasn't right with David's finances and he was going to get to the bottom of it.

CHAPTER 5: Terry

After taking care of Beast, Terry turned on his computer and pulled up the public paperwork on Maggie's divorce. Most of it was cut and dry. The assets, the little there were, had been divided and David made modest alimony and child support payments. Everything looked right, except he didn't believe it.

He searched all public records for anything about the business. Permits had been pulled. They were remodeling and they'd bought a second building.

He leaned back in his chair. That could all be attributed to an influx of cash brought on by the new wife but he didn't think that was the case. Stephanie wouldn't have married a man with no money, no matter how promising his business might be.

Something wasn't right. He'd been a divorce lawyer too long not to trust his instincts on asset hiding. This needed more investigation. He grabbed his phone, his eyes falling on the text from Maggie. Damnit. He'd completely forgotten. He looked at his watch. It was early afternoon. He'd go and see her instead of texting. His dick hardened at the thought and he almost growled. Much better than last night. Much, much better.

He called Patrick on his way to the shower. "I need you to look into the business Giving Investments and David Givens."

"Okay. Hold on. Let me write this down," said Patrick. "Anything I should know?"

He hesitated. "Yeah, it's Maggie's ex and the business that had been theirs."

"Oh. So—"

"Don't give me any shit. Just do your job."

"Ah, good to see you're back. I missed asshole Terry. Drunk Terry is a downer."

"Shut the fuck up. At least I'm not pussy whipped." He'd never, ever tell them about last night.

"I'm not either but I won't do anything that might hurt Annie." Patrick's tone was somber.

He didn't have anything to say to that.

"I'll get on it tomorrow."

"Thanks and let me know as soon as you find something."

"Will do and Terry…"

"Yeah." Now, came the meddling.

"Listen to her. I know you think you're always right—"

"I am always right."

"Okay, but sometimes there are other perspectives to consider." There was a hint of amusement in Patrick's voice. "Doesn't make you wrong but you can both be right."

"Sounds like bullshit to me."

"Think about this." Now, Patrick was annoyed. "Would you rather be right or satisfied?"

"I want both." He deserved both.

"We all do but sometimes we have to make the hard

choices." Patrick laughed. "I, for one, will choose having Annie in my arms over winning an argument every time."

"You're young and in love." He half-smiled. "Which makes you stupid."

"You think so?"

"I know so and I'm always right. Remember?" Now, he couldn't hide the smirk in his tone.

"Well, good for you. Snuggle up to that bottle of scotch again tonight or swallow your pride. Listen to what Maggie has to say. How she's feeling. Really listen and then apologize."

"I never apologize when I'm right."

"Jesus, you're worse than a child."

"Find out what you can about David Given's finances and..." Maggie wouldn't be happy with him about this.

"And?"

"I think he was having an affair before the divorce."

"Okay. I'll follow the money and have Hunter follow the body."

"Thanks." Hunter was Patrick's top guy. He swore the man could follow the scent of a scandalous thought.

"You owe me," said Patrick.

"Bill me."

"No. I'm doing this for free."

"Thanks. I guess." Now, he was nervous. None of them did much for free.

"Don't thank me yet. In exchange for this information, you need to listen to Maggie and tell her why you're really pissed."

"She knows why. She's being stubborn and stupid." But she had texted him. Maybe, she was ready to apologize and let him take care of her.

"And her not taking your money scares the shit out of you."

"No, it pisses me off because she needs it, but that's all." He broke out in a cold sweat.

"*That* sounds like bullshit to me."

"It's not."

"Terry—"

"Bill me. Because I'm not telling Maggie shit about me." He was her dom. He'd take care of her. That was all she needed to know.

"She deserves to hear why you have to control everything."

"It's who I am."

"Not who you were though."

"Jesus, Patrick. This has nothing to do with my ex."

"Doesn't it? I knew you before, remember?"

"You did investigative work for my firm. You didn't know me except as a customer."

"You don't think I do background checks on my clients?"

"Fuck." He'd never thought about it.

"You changed a lot with your divorce. Talk to Maggie about it."

"No." That was personal. Private. "It has nothing to do with me and her."

"God, you're a stubborn fool." Patrick hung up the phone.

Terry hurried into the shower. His friend was an idiot. He was who he was, talking about it wouldn't make any difference.

CHAPTER 6: Maggie

Maggie tried to keep her mind off Terry by repacking everything she'd just unpacked, but it reminded her of him. Not only because he'd helped her when she'd had no one else, but she was doing this because of him. It was over. He hadn't called or come by. He'd moved on and that made her sadder than it should've. She'd known it was a temporary thing, but she'd thought she'd have more time.

She shouldn't have texted him last night. Obviously, he wanted nothing to do with her. She grabbed her phone. She should've done this as soon as she woke but she kept hoping he'd show up or at least call. She had to salvage a bit of pride, not much, but any would help when she saw him again and she had to see him to talk about the car and the money.

She sent him another text.

MAGGIE: Last night, I wanted to ask if I could keep the car for a little while longer. Not long. I promise. I'll buy one soon. Let me know.

She sighed and put her phone on her son's bed. She grabbed a box and pulled the clothes from the drawer. She had the money to pay someone to move her things, thanks to the sale of the house. *Thanks to Terry*. But she couldn't afford to pay anyone to help her pack. She hoped Terry wouldn't make her move right away.

She'd have to return the car soon and talk to him about a payment plan for the money he'd given her to house-sit her own home. She was such a fool. How had she not suspected that it was him? No one else would do something like that. She blinked back the tears. He was a good guy—stubborn and domineering, but a good guy.

The doorbell rang. She hurried across the house. She flung open the door and her heart stopped. Terry stood on her porch—T-shirt wrinkled, hair wet like he'd just showered and he hadn't shaved. Her stomach did a somersault. He was sexy as hell and she knew how good those whiskers felt on her thighs and neck.

"You can keep the fucking car forever as far as I'm concerned."

Okay. He was a gorgeous asshole. "I can't and I won't."

"When I saw your text…the first one, I thought you'd realized how stupid you were being."

"Did you come here to insult me?" All the good feelings vanished as soon as that man opened his mouth.

"I came over because you wanted to see me." There was a slight smirk on his handsome face. "Last night. Late. I can only wonder why."

"Because we need to talk." She was not going to admit that

she'd wanted to have sex with him.

"Really?" He pulled his phone from his pocket. "At midnight?"

"Yes." Her chin jutted out.

"Sounds more like a booty call." He stepped closer, towering over her and desire flooded her veins.

"Well, it wasn't." She turned and walked into the living room. She had to put distance between them or she was going to grab him and kiss him. That'd keep his mouth shut...well, not really, but it would keep him from talking.

"Shame." He followed, closing the door behind him.

She shot him a glare. "I wanted to talk about the car and making some kind of payment plan so I can repay the money you gave me."

"What money? You refuse to trust me enough to take any. That's our problem."

"The money you gave me to watch the house."

"Oh. That's yours."

"It is not."

"It is too." His jaw was tight and his eyes narrowed. He was barely controlling his temper and she wanted to poke him until he lost it. "I paid you for a service—watching my house. Are you moving?" He looked around the room. "There are more boxes than before."

"Of course, I'm moving."

"God damnit." He ran his hand through his hair. "Stop being so fucking unreasonable."

"I'm not. You are." She closed her eyes. Now, he had her sounding like her kids. She took a deep breath. "I can't take your money and sleep with you."

"If it's one or the other, I choose sex."

"But you don't. You keep trying to give me money."

"I'm trying to take care of you."

"I don't need you to do that." But part of her wanted him too. She wanted a partner, someone to lean on.

His jaw clenched and she swore she heard his teeth grind. He took a deep breath. "Let's try again. Take off your clothes."

"What? No. We can't." But she wanted to.

His lips thinned. "Then what am I doing here?"

"I didn't text you for sex." She had and if he'd shown up last night or early this morning, she, probably, would've jumped him in the doorway.

"Right." He moved a box and sat on the couch. "Fine. Let's talk."

"Okay." She sat on the chair across from him.

"First, you enjoy having sex with me, right?"

"Yes, but—"

He held up his hand. "Let me make my case."

"This isn't court."

He shrugged. "Answer my question."

"Yes. You know I do."

"Great." He grinned. "I like having sex with you too."

Her face heated and her eyes dropped to his crotch where a large bulge was forming. When she looked up, he was watching her and his grin was even wider.

"Perhaps, we should have this discussion in bed, while I'm fucking you." He shifted as if to stand.

"No." She jumped up and moved behind the chair. She couldn't fall into his arms again. Her will power was shaky as it was.

"Okay." He leaned back on the couch and sighed. "Although, you really should consider having these conversations in bed. I'm much easier to persuade after a good fuck."

"I'll remember that."

He nodded. "Two, you need money and I have plenty. Agree?"

"I don't know how much money you have." She crossed her arms over her chest and his eyes darkened. She dropped her arms and he smiled again. The man was driving her crazy.

"Trust me, I have enough to give you what you need." He ran his hand down his thigh, drawing her gaze. "I have enough of a lot of things that you need."

She licked her lips. He sure did. She shook her head. "That may be true—"

"You know it is."

She bit the inside of her mouth to keep from laughing. He was such a male. "I'm still not taking your money."

"Damnit. I can't let you live somewhere that's unsafe, not when I can stop it."

"And I can't take your money. It'll ruin this." She waved her hand between them.

"How? I don't care about the money."

"But I do." She moved to the couch and sat next to him. "Every time you want me to do something new...in the bedroom, I'll wonder if I agreed to keep the roof over my head or money in my pocket."

"I'd never stop taking care of you because you didn't want to do something."

"You say that now, but things change. Trust me. My failed

29

marriage...your failed marriage is proof of that."

"Don't compare this to my marriage." The vehemence in his tone almost made her scoot away. "And don't compare me to that dickhead you married."

"David is not a bad guy."

"Fuck me." He stood. "He left you and his kids—his kids, not someone else's—to basically fend for yourselves. You were moving to the fucking slum because of that cocksucker."

"Not everyone has the money you do."

"Do you know where he lives?"

"Yes."

He paused. "You do?"

"I saw them the first time I went to your place."

He studied her. "So, that's why you decided to fuck me."

"Not just because of that."

"If you know where he lives then you know he's not hurting for money."

"That's Stephanie's money not his."

"Jesus, Maggie, stop sticking up for him."

"He was my husband for ten years. Yes, it's over and yes, it hurt but he'd never do anything to harm his kids."

"Un-fucking believable. Who got the money from the house?"

Her mouth opened and then shut.

"Both of you. Right? But he's doing everything he can to take care of his kids?" He paused a moment as if waiting for an answer. "That's bullshit. He has money. Stephanie is exceptionally rich. All the money from this place should've gone to you, to you and the kids."

"H-he probably didn't think about it. Or Stephanie made

him keep it." She was making excuses but she couldn't face the truth that he'd let his kids move to a bad neighborhood when he didn't have to.

"You can't be that stupid. He's a grown man. He could've done whatever he wanted with that money." He leaned down, boxing her in. "And you know what else?"

She stared at him, her eyes darting to his lips. She hated him right now and yet she wanted to pull him close and kiss him.

"I don't think he was broke when you got divorced."

"What?" There was no way that was true.

"I think your ex lied about his business. Cooked the books, so to say."

"No. David wouldn't do that."

"I think he would. I think he did."

"No." She shook her head. "He may have fallen out of love with me, but he'd never do that to his kids."

"I know Stephanie."

"You know her?" Lord help her, now she was jealous. "Did you and she..." She closed her eyes. "Sorry. That's none of my business."

"Damnit, Maggie." He shoved away and this time he stood behind the chair. "It is your business if you want it to be."

"Did you?"

"No, but I thought about it. She had her eyes out for a rich husband and I fit the bill."

"She's very pretty." Thin. Well-dressed. Sophisticated. Everything Maggie wasn't.

"She is but she's not my type."

She'd wanted him to say that Stephanie might be pretty

but she was prettier or special or something. "Right. Thin. Rich and beautiful isn't most men's type."

"She's too pushy for me. She'd never make a good sub."

Her lungs froze. He'd picked her because she was submissive. That was the only reason. "That explains a lot." She stood. She had to get out of there before she cried.

"What did I say now?"

"Nothing." She blinked back tears.

"Fuck." He stepped around the chair.

"Don't come near me."

He stopped. "What do you think I said?"

"I know what you said."

"What do you think I meant?"

"It doesn't matter."

"It sure as hell does. You're about to cry."

"I am not." She was.

"Damnit, talk to me."

"You only want me because I let you walk all over me. Boss me around. Tell me what to do."

"Maggie." He walked over to her and pulled her into his arms. "I like to be in control. I like women who like that about me. What's wrong with that?"

"Y-you won't like me if I don't do what you want. As soon as I tell you no, you'll stop wanting me."

"If that were true, I wouldn't be here right now," he said against her head.

"I meant about sex." She sobbed against his chest. He was so strong and safe. She never wanted to leave his arms.

"Any time you don't want to do something sexually with me, just tell me. My job is to take care of you. Make you happy."

"What's my job?" she mumbled against his shirt.

"To make me happy by trusting me. By listening to me."

"But I can't take your money." She cried harder. "I wish I could but I can't."

"Shhh." He stroked her hair. "We'll figure this out."

"You mean, you'll make me do what you want."

He chuckled. "You know me so well."

She pulled away, wiping at her eyes. "This isn't going to work. I'm sorry."

"Why? We both get what we want."

"You think I want your money?" She pushed his chest and stepped out of his embrace.

"I didn't mean that."

"What did you mean? Because we both get sex. I want it as much as you do."

"I doubt that."

"I don't."

His gaze heated again. "If that were true, we wouldn't be arguing right now. We'd be fucking–for the second time."

Second time? That meant the first would've been hard and fast, but this one would be slow and gloriously torturous—him bringing her to the edge and making her wait to come. Her panties dampened but she couldn't give in now. "It is true but I have standards."

"So, do I. I don't fuck any woman, only the annoying ones."

"Hey." She crossed her arms over her chest again and his eyes followed. This time, she stayed like that, letting his gaze caress her breasts. "What exactly do you get from this besides sex?"

"I get to take care of you." He moved a tiny step closer.

Her heart melted a bit, but she pushed those tender feelings away. "Not good enough."

"But it's true."

"Nope. Not enough. If I get sex and your money, what do you get?"

His eye narrowed and she swore she could see his mind spinning for an answer.

"You can cook for me."

"What?"

"Cook for me."

"I'm not that good of a cook."

His eyes sparkled and she braced herself. "Your cookies were delicious." He moved a step toward her. "All your desserts are delicious."

"I only made you cookies."

"Made? Yes, but you fed me cake with whipped cream." He licked his lips. "And cherries."

"Oh. Right." Her body was on fire. She'd missed him yesterday and by the hungry look in his eyes, he'd missed her just as much.

"You can make me little desserts that I can eat off your body. You can call them clit cakes or titty treats." He moved closer. "They can melt with heat so that the longer they're on you the harder I have to search for every last taste."

"Oh…" Her mind was fuddled with desire and memories of her splayed out on the table, him searching for his dessert.

"The chocolate cake with whipped cream was fabulous, but I'd like something with honey next time." He was right in front of her now and the heat from his body was making her tremble.

"I think you'd taste fantastic covered in honey—sticky, thick honey. Think about how long I'd have to lick to get every last drop." His hand wrapped around the back of her neck and she tipped her head, waiting for his kiss.

The doorbell rang.

"Ignore it." His lips met hers and she opened for him, wrapping her arms around his neck as he pulled her against him.

The doorbell rang again.

"Mom! Mom! Davy's puking. Open the door!" yelled Peter.

"Maggie," said David, through the door. "Sorry about bringing the kids back early but Davy's not feeling well and he wants his mom."

"I have to go." She pushed away from him and headed for the door, stopping mid-stride. "You have to leave or...or hide."

"I'm not fucking hiding again."

"Please. I don't want my kids to know."

The doorbell rang again.

"Hold on. I'm coming," she hollered.

"You will be later," he muttered. "Tell them I'm a friend."

Her eyes dropped to his pants.

"Oh. Yeah. Right." He walked toward her bedroom.

"The garage." She grabbed his arm. "You can sneak out after David leaves."

"I'm not going—"

"It'll be hours before the kids go to bed."

"Fuck." He headed for the garage. "I'll be back tonight."

CHAPTER 7: Terry

Terry tapped on Ethan's office door before walking in.

"Hey." Ethan looked up from his computer. "Didn't expect to see you tonight."

"Yeah." He walked to the couch and flopped down. He'd gotten tired of sitting at home. He'd done all the research he could on Maggie's ex. Now, it was in Patrick's hands. He glanced at his watch. The kids should be asleep soon. He shifted to take the pressure off his dick. Fuck, he wanted that woman.

"Want a drink?" Ethan moved to the bar.

"No." He was still fuzzy from last night.

"Good." Ethan smirked as he walked over to Terry and handed him a water. "I think you cleaned the Club out of scotch." He dropped down on a chair, opening his own water bottle. "Between you and Nick, I should've bought stock."

"My binge only lasted one night, so don't lump me in with Nick." His situation was completely different. He'd been upset, not pining for months over a woman.

"Right." Ethan took a gulp of his water. "You here to see

Desiree?"

"What? No."

"Hmm. Most men who've been with her are...let's say infatuated."

"She's a nice girl." He'd left her a hefty tip when he'd stopped by the bar and paid his tab, not to mention the cash he'd given her last night.

"A nice girl? She's a woman through and through."

"Yeah, but she's young." Too young for him.

"Never bothered you before." Ethan watched him closely.

"Doesn't bother me now." He couldn't afford for his friends to get even a whiff of what'd happened last night, or more accurately, what hadn't happened.

"Really?" There was a gleam in Ethan's eyes that Terry didn't like at all.

"Nope." He drank some water, plastering on his best poker face.

"But you don't want to see her again?"

"Nope." One night with a woman wasn't unusual for him.

"I understand." Ethan stretched out his legs. "She is kind of expensive for a back massage and bedtime tuck-in." His lips twitched with his effort not to laugh.

"You bastard. How..." He glanced at the other room. "You watched me on the cameras?"

Ethan roared with laughter. "I was trying to help."

"How is watching me helping?" He wanted to punch the bastard in the face. All the rooms had cameras but his friend knew he wouldn't hurt anyone, even when plastered. There'd been no reason for Ethan to watch.

"Patrick and Nick were ready to pull you out of there by

your nut-hairs. I was buying you some time."

"What the fuck?" He dropped his head on the back of the couch. "Those meddling bastards saw too?" He'd never, ever hear the end of this.

"Oh yeah. Nick, especially, can't wait to see you." Ethan laughed harder. "Gotta admit, you deserve this."

"I don't deserve shit. This is entirely different—"

"Trust me, Nick is more than ready to point out the differences. Like he was always hard for Sarah and you were…" Ethan shrugged.

"I was drunk." Fuck, they'd noticed that too.

"Right. It had nothing to do with her not being Maggie."

"Fuck no." He sat up. "It had to do with her reminding me of my daughter."

"Oh." Ethan sobered.

"Yeah. See, it's different. Entirely." It was kind of true and he was running with it.

"Hmm."

"What?" He mentally braced himself. By the look on Ethan's face, this wouldn't be good.

"I've seen pictures of your daughter and she doesn't look anything like Desiree."

"They're both about the same age."

"So, all the young women are off limits to you now?"

His eyes narrowed. He sensed a trap. "I'm not sure. I'll have to take it case-by-case."

"I'd hate to be you."

"Why?"

"Only able to get it up for old pussy." Ethan shook his head.

"There's nothing wrong with a mature woman. One who

knows the path to orgasm and loves to travel it." Like Maggie. When she came, she gave it her all.

"So, you're saying that pussy is like bread?"

"What the fuck are you talking about?"

"The more it's been pounded the softer and sweeter it is?" Ethan tried to keep a straight face but was failing miserably.

"Why are you so crass all of a sudden?" His friend usually respected women.

"One of us has to be and you've been different lately." Ethan's eyes lost all amusement as they studied him. "It's a good change. I'm happy for you. Don't fuck this up."

"This is a fling. It'll last a few months but that's it." He couldn't allow it to be anything more.

"Are you sure about that? I've seen you infatuated before but never like this."

Terry's phone beeped. Saved by the bell. "And now, I have to go." He grabbed his phone from his pocket and looked at the text as he stood. He dropped back down. "What the fuck?"

"Is everything okay?"

"Yeah. Maggie asked me not to come over." He texted her back.

"Great, we get to continue our conversation."

"Not on your life." He stood.

"Where are you going?"

"To see Maggie." He headed for the door.

"I thought she didn't want to see you."

"She does. She just doesn't realize it yet."

"Terry, don't do this. Give her time. Space. Sometimes people need room to work things out."

"That's the last thing she needs. She needs guidance not

space." His little rabbit was running but he'd hunt her down.

CHAPTER 8: Maggie

"Damn him." Maggie stared at her phone. Terry was on his way to her house. She hurried into the bathroom and brushed her teeth and hair, lecturing herself the whole time. "You are not going to see him. Okay. You'll have to see him or he'll ring the doorbell and wake the kids, but you are not going to kiss him. There's no reason to brush your teeth."

She went into her bedroom and changed her shirt but only because the T-shirt she was wearing had spittle on it. She forced herself to put on another old T-shirt. Yes, it was tight but that wasn't why she chose it.

Her phone beeped. He was almost here. She hurried to the garage, opened the door and waited in front of the car she'd borrowed from him. She was going to send him away. She really was.

His car pulled up and she bit her lip, the throbbing between her thighs insistent. He got out of the car. He looked so good in those jeans and he still hadn't shaved. She wanted him and it wouldn't hurt anyone. She could think later.

He walked into the garage. She clicked the button to close the door. He strode over to her and grabbed her chin, holding her in place for his kiss. At the first touch of his lips, she melted, her body boneless and ready for him. It seemed like it'd been forever since he'd touched her, been inside her.

"I knew you wanted to see me." He kissed his way along her face to her neck. "I just need to show you what you really want." His hand grabbed her ass and pulled her into his arms, his erection rubbing against her pussy. "Maybe, this will teach you that I know what's best for you." He nipped her neck.

"What?" Her hands slid from around his neck and down his chest, loving the play of hard muscle beneath her fingers.

"Let me show you what you want and give you what you need." He rocked against her.

She couldn't keep the soft moan inside. He felt so good, but she pushed him away. "I know what I want."

"Now, you do." He pulled her back against him. "But when I'm not touching you, you get all these stupid ideas in your head." He grinned. "I guess, I'm going to have to touch you constantly." His head dipped toward her. "It's quite a task, but I'm up to it." He rocked against her again, proving how ready he was.

"Stupid ideas?" She turned her head and he kissed her neck.

"Yeah." His hand slid under her shirt, making a slow, steady trek toward her breast.

"My ideas, my thoughts and feelings aren't stupid."

"The one telling me not to come over was." He kicked her legs apart, lifting her and sitting her on the hood of the car, her pussy flush against his swelling cock.

42

"It was not." Her mind blurred with passion as his hand shoved her bra up and his fingers teased her breast.

"It was." He bent his head, licking her nipple. "You're wet and hot for me, aren't you?"

"Yes, Sir." It came out instinctively after glorious hours of practice.

"And me not being here to fuck you, to fill that pussy and take away your ache is stupid, isn't it?" He kissed all around her nipple.

She wanted those lips on her, that mouth but it hadn't been stupid. It hadn't. "No."

"No." His eyes lifted, meeting hers as he slowly lowered his mouth.

If he took her nipple it was over. She was his. He'd win and he'd never listen to her again. Hell, he never listened to her now. "Red. Terry. Red." It was the only thing she could think of to make him stop.

He froze, his eyes widening with surprise. "Red?"

"Yes." She pulled her T-shirt down, adjusting her bra. "My safeword."

"I wasn't doing anything that—"

"I don't want you to do *anything*." She shoved at his chest, pushing him away as her unspent passion turned to anger. "I told you not to come over."

"And that was stupid. You're fucking hot for me." His eyes raked down her body. "Nipples hard. Pussy wet. For me." He took a step toward her. "You want this."

"Red." She slid off the car. "I don't. Not tonight."

"Liar." He moved closer until their bodies almost touched. "You're soaked for me."

Her breath quavered and her breasts bumped against his chest when she inhaled, making her knees shake.

"Listen to me." He grabbed her arm, steadying her, but he had an infuriating smirk on his handsome face.

"No. I'm done." She slapped at his hand and moved away, putting distance between them so she could breathe. "I need time to think."

"About what?"

"About us. This. Everything." She was falling for him, fast and hard. It was going to hurt so bad when she landed and he was gone.

"Forget about the fucking money."

"I can't." She blinked back tears. "I just can't."

"Then, cook for me." He grinned. "Clit cakes, remember?"

"No. This is...It all happened too fast. I need time. Please."

"For what? To convince yourself that it's okay to want to fuck someone? That it's okay to feel pleasure? What do you need to think about?"

"Us. I'm not the kind of woman who has flings. I married the first man I'd been serious about and stayed faithful to him for over ten years. I can't change who I am overnight."

"I'm not asking you to change. I lo...like who you are."

"But you are asking that. You're asking me to be in an arrangement with you where I take your money for sex."

"No. I'm asking you to trust me enough to allow me to take care of you. It doesn't have to be money. It can be in other ways."

"How else are you going to take care of me as a secret boyfriend?" She shook her head. "No, you don't even want that title. You're just my secret fuck-buddy."

"It's more than that and you know it." He took a step toward her. "I care about you."

Her throat filled with tears and she had a hard time swallowing. "I care about you too but I don't think I can do this anymore."

"Maggie, don't say that." He started to move toward her and stopped when she took a step back.

"Give me time, Terry. That's all I'm asking."

"How much?"

"I don't know. A couple of days. Weeks."

"Without seeing you at all?"

"Yes. I can't think when you're near me."

"Neither can I." He moved a little closer. "Come on, Maggie. Let's not think. We can figure this out together."

"But we can't. You won't let me."

"I just suggested it." The muscle twitched in his cheek.

"Because you want to force me to see things your way."

"I've never forced you to do anything."

"You're right. That wasn't the correct word. Coerced."

"I didn't do that either. You wanted everything we did."

"I did." She took a deep breath. "I need to think. Please, go." She clicked the button and the door opened.

"Damnit, Maggie."

"Please."

"Fuck." He strode out the door, his back stiff with anger.

As soon as the car left the driveway, she closed the door and sat on the floor, sobbing. She hated hurting him. All she wanted was to make him happy but she couldn't do that. He'd leave her and then she'd be miserable.

CHAPTER 9: Terry

The next few days felt like years to Terry. He'd never been so miserable or horny in his life. He wanted Maggie, no one else and he couldn't have her. He couldn't even talk to her. He glanced at his phone but Ethan's warning rang in his ear. He wasn't sure he believed giving her time would work but following his instincts had fucked everything up. So, he'd try and follow Ethan's advice.

His phone rang and he grabbed it, frowning when he saw Patrick's name.

"Hello." He didn't want to talk to anyone but Maggie.

"Hey. Got the information you wanted."

"Great. Did you email it to me?"

"Yep, but I thought I'd call. You were right, Maggie's ex hid money. A lot of money. He was also having an affair."

"I fucking knew it." He'd been a divorce lawyer too long to have been wrong.

"Great. You were right, but what are you going to do about it?"

"Take him to court. He filed false paperwork. He's going to pay, big time."

"And how long will that take?"

"A while. The courts don't move fast."

"Maggie needs money now and she doesn't need the father of her children in jail."

"It might not come to that."

"But it could. Is he good with the kids?" asked Patrick.

"Besides being okay with them moving to one of the worst areas in town? Yeah, I guess so."

"I doubt she'll appreciate you putting him in jail. She doesn't seem the type."

"I won't put him in jail. His actions and the court will do that." But Patrick was right. Maggie would not be happy about it and she'd blame him.

"Same thing."

"What do you propose I do, let him get away with it? Talk to him and ask him nicely to give Maggie the money she deserves."

"He should do that himself, but the dumb-fuck obviously won't," said Patrick.

"Nope. He won't. That's why there are courts and jails." He wouldn't lose a minute of sleep over this guy rotting behind bars.

"I have a better idea."

He leaned back in his seat. "I don't think killing him is an option we need to take. Yet."

Patrick laughed. "No. Nothing that drastic."

"What do you suggest?"

"You know Brett Mince, right?"

"The blogger? Yeah. I helped his sister with a divorce a few years back."

"And he likes to post about crappy-assed people doing shitty things, right?"

"Yeah and he's got a huge following."

"He's gotten many folks fired over stupid shit they did or said."

"Yes, he has." This was a great idea.

"I'm sure he'd like this story," said Patrick.

"If he runs with it, Maggie's ex will lose his business. His slogan is family values, honesty and shit like that."

"I know." Patrick's smug tone told him the other man had already thought this all through.

"You scare me sometimes." He grinned.

"Scare myself too, but I only use my powers for good."

"I'll call David's lawyer and schedule a meeting."

"Let me know how it goes."

"Thanks. Will do." Terry hung up and opened the file Patrick had sent him. He needed to know exactly how much to get as a one-time payment and how much to increase David's monthly child support and alimony.

CHAPTER 10: Terry

Terry sat at his house, petting Beast and waiting. He was going to see Maggie. He had a reason to, a real reason besides his desire. He'd met with her ex and she was going to get money—lots and lots of money. He couldn't wait to tell her, but if he went too early the kids would still be up. Not that he was expecting to have sex—hoping yes, but not expecting.

He looked at his watch. It was late enough. He called her. The phone rang and rang before finally going to voice mail. "Hey Maggie, it's me. I have some good news about…" If he said money, she'd immediately think he meant the money he'd tried to give her. He could explain about the information he'd uncovered about her ex but she still trusted the bastard and leaving that in a message was cruel. Nope. He'd have to tell her in person. "I have some good news," he repeated. "And I need to see you. Call me." He hung up and texted her just in case.

He ran his hand over Beast's fur and waited. And waited. And waited. He was not a patient man. When he wanted something, he went for it, always had. He texted her again.

TERRY: I'm coming over.

He gave Beast a final pat, shoved the first check from David into his pocket and hurried to his car.

As soon as he arrived at Maggie's he knew something was wrong. The house was lit like she was having a party. She wasn't, unless no one drove because there were no cars in her driveway.

He walked to the door and knocked, not wanting to wake the kids. He could hear movement and voices but no one answered. He knocked again. "Maggie, it's me. Open the door."

Nothing.

He rang the doorbell. The kids could go back to sleep.

Maggie opened the door.

"Holy crap, you look like shit."

Her hair looked like it hadn't been combed or washed in days. Her face was pale and she was wearing sweats and a T-shirt that had—he tried not to grimace—something nasty splattered all over it.

"Perfect. I feel like shit." She started to shut the door but he blocked it with his hand and pushed inside.

"You should go. We have the flu." She leaned against the wall.

The house was a disaster. The two older kids were on the couch, lying one on each end and watching cartoons. Their little faces were pale and they had big bags under their eyes. A pile of pillows and blankets lay on the floor. The baby was sound asleep on a section of them.

"All of you?" This was a nightmare.

"Yeah. It started with Davy."

"You need to go to the doctor's." He bent and lifted her. They were going to the hospital right now.

"Stop. Put me down."

"No." He turned. "Kids wrap in blankets we're going to the hospital.

"Terry, stop." Her clammy hand touched his face. "We've been to the doctor. It's the flu. We have to ride it out."

"Fuck."

"Mommy, did you hear what he said?" Peter stared at Terry like he was his hero.

"Sorry." He hadn't been around small children in years.

"Ignore him, Peter." She rested her head on Terry's shoulder. "He's going to put me down and leave."

"I'm not doing either of those things." He strode to her bedroom.

"Don't. I have to take care of the kids."

"You have to rest." He went into her room, swallowing fast because the smell of vomit almost knocked him back two feet. "Good, God."

"I tried to clean it but…"

Soiled blankets and sheets were strewn about on the floor near the bed. He looked around but couldn't find anywhere clean to put her. "The kids' rooms? Are they clean?"

"No." Tears streamed down her cheeks. "I tried but I'm so tired."

"It's okay." He sighed and held her closer.

"It's not. It's a mess."

"Shhh." He took her back into the living room and carefully

laid her on the floor. "I'll be back in a minute."

"I'm thirsty," said the little girl.

"Okay, Isabella. I'll get you something." Maggie started to get up.

He put his hand on her shoulder, stopping her. "I've got this."

"But, you don't ha—"

"Trust me." He brushed the hair away from her face. "Please. Just this one time."

She nodded, closing her eyes.

He turned to the little girl. "Can you keep liquid down?"

Isabella nodded. "I want ginger ale."

"We don't have any," muttered Maggie.

"I'll get you some water."

The little girl wrinkled her nose. "I don't like water."

"Me either," said her brother.

"Well, that's what you get and if you're good, I'll go get some ginger ale later, but only if you're good."

"And soup. Will you get soup?" asked Peter.

"We're out of that too," mumbled Maggie. "We're out of everything." She sobbed.

"Don't worry. I'll take care of it." He faced the kids. "Yes, I'll get whatever you want, but you need to be quiet and watch cartoons."

"Whatever we want?" Isabella looked at her brother, a hint of a smile on her lips.

"Yes, but only if you're good."

"We'll be good. We promise." Isabella nudged Peter.

"Yep. Real good," said Peter.

"Okay." He touched Maggie's cheek. She was burning up.

"When was the last time you took something for your fever."

"Don't know. A few hours ago, I think."

"Stay here." He walked into the kitchen. It was a disaster too with dirty dishes piled on every flat surface and the garbage overflowing but at least it didn't stink of vomit. He washed two sippy cups and put a little bit of water in them. He looked through the cabinets but there was no bread, no crackers, no soup, nothing but foods that shouldn't be given to sick children unless he wanted to clean up more puke.

He went into the living room and handed them the cups.

"I'm hungry," said the little boy.

Terry wanted to groan. Kids were a pain in the ass. "I'll get you something as soon as I have your mom settled."

"I'm fine. Take care of them."

"You are not fine lying on the floor covered in vomit."

"I'll get them something." She started to sit up, but he stopped her.

"Don't you dare move. I'll take care of this." He turned to the kids. "Being good means not complaining. You're both old enough. I'm going to let you decide."

The kids stared at him, eyes wide.

"I think that you can both wait to eat."

"But I'm hungry," said Peter.

"And your mother, the woman who takes care of you, is on the hard floor, wearing clothes that are splattered with"—he glanced at her—"either her puke or one of yours."

"His." The little girl poked her brother. "He couldn't get to the toilet."

"I tried," whined Peter.

"Do you like it when you're covered in puke?"

53

"No." Isabella looked at her brother and stuck out her chin. "We'll wait."

He smiled. "Good girl. Good boy. Watch cartoons and I promise I'll hurry."

CHAPTER 11: Terry

Terry flopped on the couch. He was beyond exhausted. He'd gone to the store, done load after load of laundry, made Maggie's bed and the kids'. He'd had the two bigger ones take baths, fed them, bathed the baby and Maggie. He'd have to do that again when she wasn't sick. His pervert of a dick hadn't cared one whit that she was ill. It'd wanted her. Still did.

He grabbed his phone from the table and texted his secretary telling her that he was going to be out of the office for a few days. Maggie wouldn't be better anytime soon—not well enough to take care of three kids. He should go home and get a change of clothes. He shut his eyes and exhaustion swept over him.

CHAPTER 12: Maggie

Maggie woke, feeling okay for the first time in what seemed like forever. She sat up and had to steady herself. She was weak but she had to check on the kids. The house was too quiet. She stood and walked down the hallway.

Isabella was in her bed, sleeping. So was Peter, but little Davy wasn't in his room. She steadied herself on the wall as she hurried into the living room. He was climbing now. If he'd gotten out of his crib...She stumbled over a toy truck on her way to the door. If he'd somehow gotten outside...She staggered to a halt. Terry was on the couch, Davy sleeping on his chest.

Her legs collapsed and she flopped onto a nearby chair. She'd forgotten about Terry. He'd shown up—she had no idea how long ago—when she'd been at her worst. The kids had been getting better but she'd wanted to die. Oh God, he'd bathed her. It shouldn't bother her. They'd done so much more together but being helpless in his arms had been different.

The poor guy had dark circles under his eyes. His hair was a mess and he looked like he hadn't shaved in days. Something nudged her arm and she jumped.

"Beast?" The dog wedged his head under her hand. Obviously, Terry had brought his dog over. He must've been here for a while. She scratched behind Beast's ear.

The house was a mess but not a disaster like it had been. Toys were scattered about but no dishes or dirty linen and best of all no lingering odor of vomit. She walked into the kitchen, Beast right behind her. It was clean. She stood in the doorway, watching Terry and her son sleep. He was so large, his legs didn't even fit on the couch, and his hand covered Davy's back entirely, but he was so good and gentle and sexier than she'd ever seen him.

She petted the dog. "Oh Beast, I'm in so much trouble." She wouldn't be able to deny him anything now. He was firmly in her heart.

CHAPTER 13: Terry

Terry woke suddenly but didn't move, conscious of the child sleeping on his chest. It felt so familiar, so right but it was terrible. He sat up, careful not to wake the baby.

"Hi." Maggie stood in the kitchen doorway, looking rumpled and tired but well.

"Hey. How are you feeling?" He placed the baby on the couch, propping pillows on the side, to keep him from falling. "Let me get you something to eat."

"I'm fine."

He walked over to her, wanting to hold her. Not fuck her, just hold her and he knew right then that he had to leave. He stopped a few feet from her. "You sure?"

She nodded her eyes warm with something he didn't want to see. "Thank you for everything."

"Yeah. No problem. If you're sure you're feeling better, I should go."

"You don't have to." She gazed at him with warmth and...God help him affection or something more.

His heart raced like he was running for his life. "I should. I haven't been to work in a few days."

"Oh, okay." The affection in her eyes was concealed now.

Shit, he was hurting her but he couldn't stop. It was better her than him.

"Okay. Bye." He hurried to the door. "See you around." Her eyes widened and he cringed. It was like he'd hit her, but coward that he was, he called his dog and almost ran to his car.

CHAPTER 14: Terry

Two days later, Terry stumbled into Ethan's office.

"Hey." Ethan looked up from his desk. "You look like shit."

"I'm feeling a bit off." He flopped onto the couch.

"Off? You're green." Ethan stood. "You need to go. I am not getting sick."

"I'm not sick. I never get sick."

"Well, buy a lottery ticket because never just arrived." Ethan pointed to the door. "Go home. Come back when you're not contagious."

He stood, pulling Maggie's check from his pocket. "Give this to Maggie for me."

"No." Ethan backed away as if Terry held a bomb. "I'm not taking anything that you touch. Go home."

"Come on. She needs the money."

"Mail it."

"That'll take days. I've had it too long already." He'd forgotten about it until he'd checked his pockets before washing his jeans.

"Then, take it to her house."

"I can't."

"Damnit, Terry." Ethan pulled the front of his shirt over his face. "If I get sick, I'm gonna kick your ass."

"Go ahead. I'd probably feel better." He held out the check again. "Do this for me. I'll owe you."

"I don't need anything except *not* to get sick. Take it to her yourself."

He dropped back onto the couch. "I can't. I can't see her anymore."

"Go away."

"I'm not leaving until you agree to take this to Maggie."

"Fuck you. Leave it on the table and go."

"You'll give it to her? Right away?"

"Yeah. I'll give it to her now. I don't want that diseased thing in my office any longer than it has to be."

"Thanks." Terry stood.

"Fuck you, patient zero."

Terry left the check and went home to crawl into bed and die.

CHAPTER 15: Terry

Terry felt like he'd just fallen asleep when his doorbell rang. "Go away," he shouted but it came out a raspy whisper. His throat was dry and he hurt everywhere—his head, his body, even his hair ached. He dropped back onto the pillow. Whoever was there would leave.

The doorbell rang again. He pulled the pillow over his head. It rang again and again and again.

"Fuck me." He stood, swaying a bit as he staggered through his house. "No, fuck you." He yanked open the door.

Maggie stared up at him, frowning. She looked great—clean and soft and she smelled fresh, unlike him who reeked of sweat.

"Oh, Terry." The anger on her face faded as she stepped toward him, feeling his forehead. "You're sick. You need to be in bed." She grabbed his arm, her hand cool on his hot skin. "You're burning up." She took him to the couch. "Sit."

"Bed." He wanted to go to bed.

"No. I can't take care of you here. I'm going to pack some

clothes and you're coming to my house."

"No. I'm fine. I just need sleep."

"You are not fine." Her hands were on her hips and her breasts jiggled with the tapping of her foot. "You need water." She touched his forehead again. "When was the last time you had something to drink?"

He shrugged. He had no idea.

"You're coming with me."

"No." But she was already on her way to his room. He started to follow but dropped back onto the couch, stretching out. He was so fucking tired. "Need to sleep." His eyes closed and it seemed like a second later she was tugging on his hand.

"Come on."

"Go away," he mumbled.

"You can sleep as soon as you get to my place."

"I'm not going anywhere. Go home." He couldn't deal with her right now.

She blinked back tears and then straightened. "I came by to thank you for everything you did. David. The check. The additional child support and alimony."

"No problem." He closed his eyes. "Goodbye, Maggie. Have a nice life."

She turned and hurried to the door, her footsteps making a soft pat on his carpet. He threw his arm over his face as the door closed. He was a bastard for hurting her like that but he couldn't do it again. He'd never survive.

CHAPTER 16: Maggie

Maggie sat in her car...no, Terry's car and cried. She had no idea what'd happened. Maybe, he only wanted women who needed him, depended on him for everything. Now that she had money, she only needed him for her heart and body, not to support her.

It didn't make sense. He'd stayed at her house and had cared for her and the kids. They were still asking for Mister Terry. This was what she hadn't wanted to happen. He'd not only hurt her but her kids too. It was over. Done. She wasn't letting anyone hurt her children.

She started the car and drove home. She was done with him, with men, but he was so sick right now. She knew exactly how miserable he must feel. His entire body had to hurt and not getting enough fluids wouldn't help. He needed water with that fever. She pulled into her driveway and hurried into the house.

"Kids, pack your bags. We're going to stay with Mister Terry." She shooed the babysitter out, paying her a little extra since she hadn't been able to all those months.

"Is everything okay, Mrs. Givens?" asked Tina.

"A friend of mine is sick. Flu like we had. We'll be gone a few days. I'll call you when we get back."

As soon as she had all their bags packed, she drove to Terry's house. She hadn't locked the door behind her and he probably hadn't moved from the couch. She was going to stay until he was well and then she'd leave and never look back.

CHAPTER 17: Terry

Terry had to be dreaming. No, he was having a nightmare because through his door came Maggie and her kids. Everything he feared was walking straight toward him.

Beast, the traitor, trotted over to them, tail wagging.

Peter ran to the couch. "Mister Terry, are you sick? Mommy says you're sick."

"I am and I want to sleep. Tell your mommy to take you home."

The little boy dropped down on the couch by him. "You never took us for pizza. You promised."

His stomach twisted at the thought of that greasy, cheesy dish and he clenched his jaw. He hadn't thrown up yet and he had no intention of changing that.

"Peter, don't talk about food. Mister Terry's belly hurts." Maggie took his hand. "Come on, Mister Terry." She grinned at his glare. "Let's get you to bed."

"Go away," he said under his breath.

"As soon as you're well, I'll leave and never see you again."

He stood. That was the last thing he wanted but it was what had to be. "Promise?" He was being an ass but he had to chase her away now. If he didn't, it'd destroy him when she left and she would leave. No woman like her, kind and caring, would put up with his shit for long.

She straightened her shoulders. "I promise."

He let her lead him into his bedroom and he dropped onto his bed. "I feel better already. You can go now."

"Take a shower and change your clothes. I'll be back to check on you after I make some soup." She hurried out of the room.

He buried his face in his pillow. He was a dick. There were tears in her voice and he'd put them there.

CHAPTER 18: Maggie

Maggie hurried into the bathroom by the living room, closing the door behind her. She sat on the side of the tub and let the tears fall. She hadn't thought Terry was a cruel man. She'd been wrong, but it didn't matter. He'd helped her a lot and she'd repay him by taking care of him until he was well. Then, she'd leave and move on with her life. She wiped her face and walked into the living room. She put the TV on for the kids, retrieved the playpen from the car, set it up near the couch, deposited Davy in there with some toys and went into the kitchen.

She made some soup from a box that she'd brought with her and took a snack to the kids. "Mommy is going to be in the back with Mister Terry. You guys be good. If you need anything come and get me."

"Okay," said the two older kids, eyes glued to the television.

She took the soup, crackers and some water into his room. He was still stretched out on the bed in his dirty clothes. She wasn't surprised. He'd never listened to her before, he wasn't going to start now. She put the tray on his dresser and went back to the kitchen. She grabbed a clean, large pan and walked into the master bathroom. She half-filled the pan with warm, soapy water, tossed in a washcloth and carried it into his bedroom. She dug through his dresser until she found some sweatpants and a clean T-shirt. She tossed them on the bed and sat down.

"Terry. Terry." She shook him.

"Go away." He buried his face in the pillow.

"Not until you're cleaned and fed."

"I'm not a child."

"Then, stop acting like one."

He rolled over, glaring at her.

She pushed his shirt up and he lifted so she could remove it. She took the cloth from the bowl and began to skim it over his torso. He was so strong and lean, his chest wide with a sprinkling of dark hair that formed a V straight to his crotch. She tried not to look. She knew too well what lived between his legs and she missed it.

She raised his arm, washing him. Luckily, his eyes were closed. She leaned in lifting him as much as she could to get his back, her breasts pressing against his chest. She bit her lips as her nipples hardened from the contact. It was embarrassing how desperate she was. The man had the flu and still her body craved his.

Her hands went to his jeans.

"Don't." His eyes opened.

"You'll be more comfortable in sweats."

"I'll be more comfortable if you stop touching me."

She swallowed the lump of hurt and anger. "I will but you have to wash and dress yourself." She threw the clothes she'd grabbed for him in his face and stood. "I'll be back in ten minutes. If you're not dressed, I'll do it."

"Fuck this." He started taking off his pants.

She stepped outside, closing the door and leaning against it. He was such an ass. She wiped her eyes. As soon as he was even a little better, she was gone.

CHAPTER 19: Terry

The next few days were a blur to Terry. The only thing he remembered was that Maggie was always there. It was heaven and hell because he couldn't do anything but appreciate her fingers skimming over his hot flesh and her scent surrounding him. He was too weak to touch her like he craved, to kiss her and to fuck her. Even his dick was too tired to respond. It'd twitch every now and then but standing tall was too much for it.

He rolled over, tossing the covers aside. He wasn't hot anymore. His fever had broken and his body, although still tired, didn't feel like it was beyond living. He sat up, drinking the water that was in a cup on his nightstand. It was delicious, like nectar from the gods, and he had Maggie to thank. She really was a natural caregiver. He'd been sick and grumpy and she'd been pleasant and attentive, but most important she'd stayed.

He stood and went into the bathroom, starting his shower. He needed it bad. He stared in the mirror, barely recognizing the man who looked back at him. His face was gaunt and pale, big bags under his eyes and he had a decent beard going. He scratched his jaw. He needed to shave and lord help him, brush his teeth. He grabbed his toothbrush and had just put it in his mouth when Maggie stepped into the bedroom.

"Terry? You're up. How are you feeling?" She touched his head. "Fever's gone."

He pulled out the toothbrush. "Better. Thanks."

"I'm glad." She turned and started to leave.

"I'll be out after I shower."

She glanced at him over her shoulder and gave him a slight nod.

The shower was fabulous. The hot water soaked into his body, soothing away the aches. He stayed in there a long time, but not only because it felt good. He wasn't ready to face Maggie. There was no way he could let her go. She'd cared for him and even though his instincts screamed at him to push her away before she hurt him, he couldn't. Not now.

He turned off the shower and got out, drying and putting on clean clothes. He walked down the hallway. The house was quiet. It hadn't been quiet in days—always in the background had been kids and television and laughter. All the sounds he'd loved and lost when his wife had left him.

His feet froze when he stepped into the living room. They were gone, all of them. Just like before, nothing remained but pain and memories.

CHAPTER 20: Terry

Terry sat in his office staring out the window. The last two weeks had been terrible. He didn't want to do anything. Everything was routine and unappealing. He woke, took care of Beast and went to work, where he sat. Nothing sparked his interest or motivated him.

After work, he'd go home. He didn't even go to the Club anymore. There was no point. He didn't want any of those women. He wanted Maggie. Ethan and the others had called him numerous times, trying to get him to come by for poker or something, but he'd declined every time, making up excuse after excuse. He'd have to go there soon; they were threatening to bring the game to his house and then he'd never get rid of them. At least at the Club, he could stay for an hour and leave— go home to his empty house and sleep. If it weren't for Beast, he might never get up again, but the dog needed him. At least, someone in his life did.

The intercom buzzed.

"Yes?"

"There's a Sarah Daly to see you, sir."

She was probably here to bitch at him. Even though he hadn't been to the Club, he'd been calling Nick and hounding him about the prenup. He had to get his friend to sign one. Nick was innocent in the ways of the world. He'd never been really hurt and Terry had to protect him from as much of it as was possible. He'd start by dealing with the bitch Nick was going to marry. "Send her in." Finally, there was something that interested him—saving his friend.

He put the papers that he'd been pretending to study aside. Sarah walked in. He stood. He didn't want to but it was an ingrained reaction when a woman entered the room. "Sarah."

"Terry." She strolled across the office, her long, lean legs making short work of the space. She was an attractive woman but he didn't like her. She was going to end up crushing his friend and that made her his enemy.

"Please, have a seat." He motioned to the chair in front of his desk.

"Thank you." She sat.

"Would you like something to drink?" He could use a stiff shot, but it was too early for that unless she wanted one.

"No, thank you." She pulled two large, manila envelopes from her purse.

Damn. The woman couldn't even be accommodating about that. He sat. "So, what brings you here"—he glanced at the door—"without Nick?" He wanted to make it clear, if it wasn't already, that he was Nick's friend.

"I'd like you to look over the prenup my lawyer prepared for me." She handed him one of the envelopes.

"You have a prenup?" This was just perfect. She was

protecting her assets but Nick's were hanging free and unprotected like a naked man in a knife factory.

"Yes." She crossed her legs and studied him. "I know you don't like me and you blame me for Nick's refusal to sign a prenup—"

"Obviously, he's not refusing to sign yours, is he?" He pulled the papers from the envelope.

"He's agreed to sign whatever I give him."

"Stupid bastard."

"Exactly."

"If you want me to tell him to sign this"—he waved the documents in the air—"you're in for a surprise. I'm not fucking-over my friend."

"Are you done?" There was a hint of amusement in her green eyes.

"No, I'm not done." He tossed the papers on his desk. "This is ridiculous. It proves that you only want his money and that—"

"Stop throwing a fit and look at it before you condemn me."

He stared at her, disliking her more than his ex-wife right now and that was saying a lot.

"Please." She pushed the papers across his desk.

He grabbed them and starting reading. He glanced up at her. "Your lawyer wrote this? A lawyer you paid?"

"Yes. She wasn't very happy about it either."

"Hmm." This didn't make sense. He finished the document. He should keep his big mouth shut, but..."Do you understand what this says? What will happen if you and Nick get divorced."

"Yes." A bit of doubt crept into her eyes.

"You could lose everything. Everything you have now and

everything you make in the future." There was no way she understood that. No way.

"I know."

"Why?" None of this made any sense. She was after Nick's money. She had to be. It was what women did. They promised to love a man and then they changed their minds, taking half of what he made, what he'd worked forever for, along with things that couldn't be replaced, like kids and a home and companionship.

"Nick refuses to let you write a prenup. I know you think it's me who doesn't want one, but you're wrong." Her lips twisted into a half smile. "Nick is a bit naïve about life."

His eyebrows shot up. He thought that too, but he'd had no idea she did. Nick and naïve were not two words that normally came out of a woman's mouth.

"I don't know how much you know about my past."

"Not much."

"So, you weren't privy to my background check?"

"No. I'm Ethan's lawyer not his private investigator."

"It's nice to know that not everyone at the Club is told everything."

"Ethan is very serious about his business."

"Believe me, I know that." She smiled and Terry almost smiled back. There was something charming about her. Her smiled faded. "I lost someone a long time ago. He...he fell out of love with me. It happens and it's no one's fault."

He didn't agree with that. If a person made a commitment, they stuck with it. Worked at it. They didn't leave and take the kids, take his family.

"I didn't understand that at the time. I don't think any of us

76

do if we're the one left behind. It causes us—well me, anyway—to make bad decisions. Decisions based on anger and hurt. Decisions that we aren't proud of later but have to live with."

"If you did something illegal, don't tell me. I'm not your lawyer."

She smiled sadly. "I wish it were something like that but it was worse." Her eyes were filled with a sorrow that he couldn't even comprehend. "I was pregnant and when he left me, I hated him and our baby."

"A lot of women have abortions."

"I thought about it, but then Adam died. That baby was all that was left of him in this entire world, but it was too late." She looked down at her hands. "I lost it."

"I'm so sorry." He'd had no idea about any of this.

"They say it was the stress but I can't help feeling that if I'd wanted that baby, loved it, it would've lived."

"I'm sure that's not the case."

She wiped her eyes and looked at him. "Probably not, but it's how I feel and that's why I want to make sure that Nick is protected." She took a deep, shaky breath. "If he leaves me or cheats on me five years, ten years down the road, I'll be so hurt and angry that I may do something I'll regret like take him for every penny I can. This will protect him and me."

"This"—he tapped the papers—"is not protecting you." He was still on Nick's side, but he didn't want to see her do anything stupid either.

"But it is. It's protecting me from a lifetime of regrets."

"Oh, I think you'll regret signing this if you and Nick separate."

She laughed a little. "Probably, but not as much as doing

77

something that will cause me to hate myself years later." She handed him the other envelope. "I'm hoping that when Nick sees the prenup I gave you first, you can convince him to sign this one instead."

Here it came. The prenup that'd ruin Nick's life. She was good. Her sob story had gotten to him, but he'd heard a lot of sad stories in his career. He'd never let them affect his judgement. He took the papers from the envelope and skimmed over them. "These protect what you have now but anything you make in the future will belong to both of you. If these are signed, you can still take half of everything Nick has now and later."

"I want you to draw up a prenup for Nick, protecting his current assets."

"Already done." He pulled some papers from his desk. "The dumbass won't sign them."

She took the papers from him and read them. "May I have a pen?"

"Sure." He handed one to her. "You may want your lawyer to look these over before..."

She signed and handed them back to him. "I'm quite familiar with contracts and unfortunately, now prenups."

He stared at the papers. She was for real. She didn't want Nick's money; she just wanted Nick.

She stood. "Please, get Nick to sign the second prenup."

"I could give him the first and screw you over big time."

Her eyes gleamed with amusement. "Nick wouldn't do that to me. Plus, I haven't signed them yet."

He glanced at the last page and smiled. "Smart girl."

"At least, not stupid." She grinned.

"Sarah, I can honestly say that it's been a pleasure." He stood and held out his hand.

"Same here." She shook it.

He sat down but she didn't leave. "Is there something else?"

"Starting over, letting someone else get close after losing everything is hard, but it's worth it."

"I'm glad you're better." He didn't think she was just talking about herself.

"It took work, but staying home alone with my dog, although I do love Tank, wasn't enough for me." Her gaze drifted over his face. "Or for anyone. Take a chance. Sometimes people surprise us." She turned and stopped at the door. "Oh, we'll be at the Club tonight. Can you bring the papers by then?"

"I wasn't planning on going to the Club tonight."

She frowned. "Please. I'd like to get this prenup stuff behind us and"—she flushed a little—"Nick is going to feel the need to punish me after this and we'll be in the perfect place."

He laughed. "I'll be there." Nick was a lucky man. He felt the need to punish a certain woman, but she wanted nothing to do with him any longer.

CHAPTER 21: Maggie

Maggie stepped out of Annie's car and tugged on her skirt. It was tight and short—mid-thigh—but she wasn't used to dressing like this. "I don't think this is a good idea."

"Nonsense," said Annie. "You look amazing."

"I'm not sure about that either." She wore a new black skirt, a flouncy, white blouse that showcased her breasts and showed more cleavage than she was comfortable with displaying, and black high heels.

"Trust me. Terry is going to burst when he sees you." Annie grinned as she took Maggie's arm and headed toward the garage entrance to La Petite Mort Club. "Poor man's probably close to bursting now. He hasn't been to the Club. That means, more than likely, he hasn't been with anyone since the two of you broke up."

"I wouldn't call it breaking up. We weren't exactly going out." They'd just been having sex...lots and lots of sex.

"Doesn't matter what you call it. He's going to flip when he sees you."

Maggie touched her hair. "Are you sure about the ponytail? It seems so childish." She often wore her hair tied back at home, but the Club was filled with rich, elegant, well-dressed people.

Annie's eyes gleamed with amusement. "Trust me. There's nothing childish about a ponytail in a place like this."

"What do you mean by that?" She started to wonder if her friend was leading her down a path she didn't want to go.

"I guess you're right."

"About what?" She followed Annie to the doors of the Club.

"If you and Terry had been going out, you'd know exactly what a ponytail does to a guy like him." Annie nodded at the bouncer. "This is my friend, Maggie. Ethan approved her visit."

The bouncer checked his phone and said, "Have fun, ladies." He stepped aside and Maggie found herself once again in the Club.

It wasn't as crowded as the other night, but there were still plenty of people. She stopped. A woman was on a stage, tied up and being whipped with a small flogger. "Oh my." God help her, she was getting wet.

"I know." Annie stared openly. "I love this place." She took Maggie's arm. "But let's get a drink."

"I'm going to need it." If Terry didn't show or didn't want her, she wasn't sure what she'd do. She might be able to pick up someone else. She was horny enough and the kids were with their father this weekend, but she truly wasn't a casual sex kind of woman.

Annie ordered their drinks. When the bartender delivered them his eyes skimmed over Maggie's cleavage, making her blush.

"I told you that you look great." Annie grinned.

"Men like boobs."

"Yes, they do." Annie tugged her shirt down a little, highlighting her own nice sized breasts.

Maggie glanced around sipping her rum and coke. "What if he doesn't show or doesn't want anything to do with me?"

"He'll show. Sarah took care of that and as for the other"—Annie looked her over—"that's not possible."

But it was. Terry had made it clear when he'd been sick that he didn't want her anywhere near him. "This is stupid. I should go." She put down her drink.

"No. Wait. Give it some time. Plus"—Annie's eyes landed on someone and she smiled—"it doesn't hurt to look."

A handsome, older man, probably in his late fifties or early sixties, headed their way. He stopped in front of them. "Annie." He leaned down and gave her a quick kiss on her cheek.

"Richard." Annie kissed him back. "Nice to see you again."

"Can I be so lucky to have you here without your hulking sidekick?" His eyes raked over Annie.

Annie laughed. "Patrick will be here soon and you know me, Richard. I don't do anything except with Patrick."

"Shame." His eyes drifted to Maggie. "I don't believe I've met your friend."

Annie turned. "Maggie, this is Richard and Richard this is Maggie. She's currently unattached."

"Really?" His eyes roamed over her body, lingering for one hot moment on her chest. "Unbelievable."

Part of her wanted to put her hands over her cleavage, but another part was flattered. David had been wrong. Even after having three kids and gaining some extra pounds, she was still an attractive woman. "I'm waiting on someone but I don't know if he'll be here tonight."

"His loss." Richard moved closer. "I'd love to show you around the Club."

"Maybe later," interrupted Annie. "We want to give Terry a little time to make the right decision."

"Terry? He's the one you're waiting for?" asked Richard.

Maggie nodded. This was going to be even more embarrassing if Terry ignored her or arrived with someone else.

"I haven't seen him here in weeks." Richard's gaze darkened. "This may be my lucky night after all."

Maggie couldn't stop a tiny smile. Annie hadn't fibbed. Terry hadn't been here with all these beautiful women. It still didn't mean he wanted her or was waiting for her, but it did help.

"He'll be here tonight," said Annie.

"That's a shame. I think, until he does arrive"—Richard moved a little closer to Maggie—"we should get to know each other better." He touched her ponytail, giving it a little tug. "I'd like that. Wouldn't you?"

CHAPTER 22: Terry

Terry sat in Ethan's office watching Nick fume. He couldn't help it; he was enjoying this. The younger man was a fool in love and he was damn lucky to have fallen for someone like Sarah. He glanced at her. She was calm and composed while Nick ranted.

"Damnit Sarah, I'm not signing this." He threw the papers on the table. "We don't need a prenup."

"I do." She stared up at him from the couch. "I need one. I need you to sign one."

He squatted in front of her. "My parents didn't have one. Your parents didn't have one."

"Our parents married when they were younger, just starting out. They had nothing to protect."

"I'm not signing it."

"Then, I'll sign and file the first one. Since it has nothing to do with your assets, I don't need your signature." Her jaw took on a stubborn tilt.

"No." Nick stood. "That'll leave you with nothing."

"Nick, sign the damn prenup." He took a sip of his scotch. "She's got you neatly backed in a corner."

"Shut the fuck up, Terry. This is your fault."

"Oh no. You aren't blaming me for this." He tipped his glass at Sarah. "She came up with this brilliant plan all on her own."

"Sarah..." Nick glared at her before storming away.

"I'm doing this for us." She walked over to him, her hand running up and down his back. "Please. Sign the papers. This'll protect both of us."

Nick turned to face her. "I'm marrying you forever. Don't you feel the same?"

"I do." She stood on tiptoe and kissed him. "But things can change."

"I won't stop loving you."

"I know." She kissed him again, but this one was a little longer and deeper. "Then, this will all be for nothing. It doesn't hurt either of us to have them."

Nick took a deep breath. "Fine, but you'll pay for making me do this."

"I was counting on that." She grinned.

Terry looked away, the love and devotion on their faces making him sick with envy.

Nick scratched his name on the papers and so did Sarah. Ethan and Patrick signed as witnesses.

"Good. That's done." Sarah's lawyer took her set of the papers. "I'll file these on Monday."

"Agreed." Terry slid his copies of the documents into his briefcase.

She stood. "Goodnight."

"You're welcome to stay and enjoy the Club." Ethan's gaze

took in the lawyer's long legs and slender form.

"Thanks. I may take you up on that, but first, I want to take these to my office." She tapped her briefcase.

"Hope to see you later," said Ethan.

She smiled at him as she left.

It looked like Ethan's night was planned. He hadn't felt like sticking around to play cards anyway. He stood. "Well, that's enough for me. Goodnight."

"You're leaving?" Ethan turned on the monitors that showed him the Club.

"Yep."

"It's Friday night," said Sarah.

"So." He was in no mood to be around the couples or go into the Club.

"Ah, Annie's here." Patrick moved closer to the screen.

"That's wonderful." Why the fuck did he care? He started for the door.

"She brought a friend," said Patrick.

"Good for her. You guys are finally going to do a ménage. Great. Have fun."

"Oh, I don't think that's in the cards, but this lady might be in for some punishment." Patrick grinned. "Her hair is in a ponytail."

"Fabulous." He hesitated at the door. They were all looking at him. Something was wrong.

"You may want to check out Annie's friend." Patrick gave him a smug look.

"You didn't." He strode across the room to the monitor. "Sonofabitch." It was Maggie. "You brought her here?"

"I didn't." Patrick backed away, hands up by his chest.

"Annie did but Maggie wanted to come. It seems she got a taste of kink and wants more." He grinned. "I wonder who can help her with that?"

"It fucking won't be Richard." The other man was at the bar talking to the women. He was a suave, sophisticated, rich bastard. One of Terry's good friends but Richard was not getting his hands on Maggie.

CHAPTER 23: Maggie

Maggie laughed and sipped her drink. Richard was charming and attractive. It was flattering that he was interested in her, but he wasn't Terry. She scanned the Club, feeling a little guilty for not giving Richard her full attention, but her heart and body wanted Terry.

Richard's grin widened and he leaned down, his lips almost touching her ear. "I think you're in for a night you won't soon forget, little Maggie-May."

"Get the fuck away from her." Terry's words were low and dangerous.

Maggie jumped, her entire body tingling at the sound of his voice.

"Terry, how nice of you to join us." Richard straightened.

"She's mine." Terry stepped closer.

Richard grinned, a hint of fire in his grayish-blue eyes. "That's for the lady to decide."

Both men looked at her.

"Ah..." She had no idea what to say. She wanted Terry but

he'd ignored her. He'd sent her away.

"Tell him that you're with me," ordered Terry.

Annie grabbed her arm, pulling her close. "Don't make it too easy on him."

Terry glanced to the side. "Patrick, get your woman out of my way."

Patrick walked up and leaned against the bar. "Annie will decide when she's ready to go."

Annie grinned at her boyfriend. "Have I told you how much I love you?"

"Not today." Patrick's eyes roamed over her and Maggie almost fanned herself. "Worse yet, you haven't shown me since this morning."

"We can't have that." Annie hugged Maggie. "Make him suffer but not too much. He's hurting too." She took Patrick's hand. "Let's go."

The two wandered away, heading toward the playrooms.

"You seem curious about those rooms," said Richard. "I'd love to show you exactly how much pleasure can be had back there."

"That's not going to fucking happen." Terry grabbed her arm, pulling her to his side. "She's with me."

"Am I?" She jerked free.

"Yes." His face was tight with anger.

"You told me to go away." Even saying those words hurt.

"I didn't tell you to come here." He stepped forward, boxing Richard out of the conversation. "What in the fuck are you doing here?"

She shrugged. Looking for him wasn't the right answer. It was the truth, but she wasn't admitting that, at least not yet.

"Well, you're leaving."

"I am not." She crossed her arms over her chest. This man drove her crazy. She loved and hated his domineering ways.

"Seems, Maggie-May wants to stay and play." Richard moved back to her side.

"I'm not kidding, Richard. Leave us alone."

"I need to hear it from the lady first." Richard looked down at her expectantly.

She frowned at Terry and turned to Richard, a smile spreading across her face. "Thank you for the drink, but I do have some things to discuss with Terry." She looked over her shoulder at him, letting the smile drop and then turned back to Richard. "Maybe when we're done, I'll find you."

Terry muttered a slew of curse words.

Richard grinned. "Absolutely. If Terry can't satisfy your...curiosity, come find me. I'll be happy to help."

"You heard her. Now, go." Terry grabbed her arm. "Or better yet, we'll go." He walked toward the door.

"Wait." She stumbled after him, her short legs no match for his long ones. "Stop." He wasn't listening again. "Red."

That did it. He halted midstride, looking down at her. "You can't keep using that for no good reason."

"I'd stop using it if you'd listen to me just once."

"I'm listening." But from the look on his face, he wasn't happy about it.

She gazed up at him. He was so mad and yet she felt safe with him. He'd never hurt her, not physically anyway, and she wanted him bad enough to risk the emotional pain of him leaving her. "I want to stay here and explore."

CHAPTER 24: Terry

Terry's dick was beyond hard. His little rabbit wanted to play, but no matter what she said, Maggie wasn't ready to play at the Club. It'd be weeks, maybe months, before he'd take her to a playroom. "Trust me. You don't want to stay here."

"I'm not going home and spending the weekend alone."

She was trying so hard to be brave, his little rabbit. He stepped closer to her, letting her feel the heat from his body, the way he was so much bigger and stronger than she was. "Do you want to go to a stage?" He let his eyes dart to one of the platforms on the Club floor. "I can tie you up and do whatever I want to you."

She stared at one of the scenes unraveling on a small stage. The woman was naked, a ball gag in her mouth and her large breasts swinging as her dom fucked her from behind.

"Is that what you want?" He whispered in her ear. "To be seen by everyone while I fuck you?"

She shook her head but her tongue darted across her lips. He bit back a moan. He needed that tongue on his cock.

"Answer me, rabbit. You know the rules, shaking your head doesn't count."

"No. I don't want that."

"I think you do." He stepped closer until his chest pressed against hers. "Or is it only part of that you desire?"

Her gaze was locked on the couple.

"We could go to a back room." His hands, unable to not touch her, stroked up and down her arms. "But there are cameras there."

Her gaze snapped to his. "Cameras? You mean people are watching"—her eyes darted to the couple in the middle of the room—"even in the private rooms?"

"Especially, in the private rooms. Safety and all. You understand."

"Oh." Her face fell a bit. "I don't want to be on camera."

"Then, we go." His hand grasped hers. "To my house."

"To your house?"

"Yes." He pressed his lips against her ear. "Where I can do whatever I want to you. Where no one is watching and no one will stop me." He held his breath, waiting for her reply. She should know by now that he'd never hurt her, but she was taking a chance. Hell, he was taking a chance.

"Okay." The word was a breathless whisper.

He wanted to pound his chest in triumph but he reined it in. "I have to warn you, rabbit. If you come home with me, I may never let you leave." He wasn't sure he was strong enough to walk away again. Hurt or not, he needed her.

"So, I'd be your sex slave? Tied to your bed and at the mercy of your desire?" Her eyes sparkled with humor and passion.

"Yes." His lips brushed against hers.

"On one condition."

"What?" He didn't like conditions.

She touched her hair. "You tell me what's so special about a ponytail."

"I'll do more than tell you." He grabbed her hand. "I'll show you." He headed toward the elevator fast because this first time tonight, he wasn't going to last long.

CHAPTER 25: Maggie

Maggie followed Terry through his garage, both nervous and excited.

He opened the door to the house. "After you."

She went inside, bending to pet Beast.

Terry's hand landed on her ass, squeezing. "I like the skirt."

She straightened, wiggling her butt. "You don't think it's too tight?"

"Not at all." He rubbed her cheeks. "Covers too much, maybe, but not too tight."

"Hmm." She leaned against him and his lips touched her neck.

"I'm not going to last long, Maggie. Not this time." His dick pressed against her. He was fully aroused.

"Good. Neither will I." She tipped her head and met his lips. "It's been too long."

His eyes darkened as he spun her around, pulling her into his arms as his mouth devoured hers. His kiss was dark and hot, almost as desperate as she felt. One of his hands cupped her ass, holding her against his erection. God, she'd missed this, missed him. His other hand grasped her breast, making her moan as he pinched her nipple.

He broke away, stepping back. "Go to the bedroom. Now." He was almost panting.

"Yes, Sir." She couldn't stop the shiver that raced through her at his snarl. She hurried into his bedroom, stopping at the bed and waiting for his command.

He stood in the doorway, his dark eyes raking over her body. "Fuck. I want to do so many things to you."

She wanted that too. She was ready to surrender to him. Let him do whatever he wanted. "I have all weekend."

He unbuttoned his pants. "That's a start."

A start? Oh, praise the lord, she was in for a good weekend.

"Go to the foot of the bed."

She strolled over, letting her hips sway, and then started to climb on it.

"Stop. Did I tell you to get on the bed?"

Now, she was confused. "No, Sir." She started to turn toward him.

"Face the bed."

"Okay." She did. "Sorry, Sir. I thought—"

"Don't think. That's my job." He moved closer and kissed her neck. "Your job is to feel." His hands ran down her front, teasing her nipples.

"Yes, Sir." She could do that. She lifted her arms, wrapping them around his neck while he kissed her and played with her breasts through her shirt. She wanted to take it off, feel his skin on hers but he was in charge.

He took one of her hands and placed it on the bed post, wrapping her fingers around it. "Hold on."

She did.

"Stay right there." He walked to his closet and came back holding something that was long and black, rope-like.

"What's that?" Her voice quavered. He was going to tie her up. She'd be completely at his mercy. A surge of desire dampened her panties.

"Restraints." He took her wrist, wrapping the Velcro around it and pulling it tight. "How's that feel?"

"Okay." It was tight but it didn't hurt.

"Let me know if you need it loosened." He hooked the other side to her other wrist. He took off his shirt, tossing it on the floor before reaching around her and wrapping the excess length of the restraint around first one bed pole and then the other. He used a sliding device to tighten it until her arms were spread wide.

Her heart raced. She couldn't move her hands. She couldn't stop him from doing whatever he wanted. She tugged as he stepped to the side, his eyes meeting hers. He was all hot muscle and strength and she was his prisoner, his captive. The wetness almost ran from between her legs. She'd never been so turned on in her life.

"Like this, don't you?" His eyes were on her breasts.

She glanced down and her nipples were so hard that they poked through her bra and showed through her shirt. "Yes." There was no point lying. He could see the proof.

He moved behind her, his hands running up under her shirt. He unhooked her bra. "Should've done this before I tied you up. Oh well." He walked back to the closet. He came back with scissors.

"Terry, what are you doing? This is a new shirt and bra."

"You should've thought of that before you came to the Club."

The cold steel of the scissors skimmed up her arm and down her side. She shivered. "Terry, don't. Just take my arms down. We can remove my clothes and then hook me back up."

"Nope." He nipped her neck. "You came to the Club and teased me. Pranced around, flirting with Richard. You knew you were mine." He began cutting the other side of the shirt.

"I didn't."

He yanked and the shirt was gone. He tossed it on the bed. It was ruined, cut into pieces.

"Damnit. What am I going to wear now?"

"Nothing." His hands held her bra strap. "You're my naked prisoner. You agreed when we left the Club." The scissors snipped and he dropped the strap.

"I didn't agree to you ruining my clothes."

"You didn't say I couldn't." He turned her face and kissed her, his lips hard on hers. He broke away. "And you never said your safeword." He cut the other strap and tossed the bra by the shirt.

"Ah…" She hadn't. She could've, but she didn't.

He moved to the side, looking her over like a predator eyes his cornered prey.

Her nipples were hard little pebbles and she shivered. A little cold without his body heat.

"Restraints good?"

She tugged on them again. "Yeah."

"Excellent." He kicked off his shoes and pulled off his socks.

He stepped onto the bed, the bulge in his pants right in front of her face.

Her eyes locked on his cock and she licked her lips. She couldn't help it. He was so big.

"Have you been with anyone since me?" He rubbed his dick through his pants.

"No."

"Good." He unzipped his pants, shoving them and his underwear down. He hadn't been kidding, he was beyond ready, already dripping. "Open." He guided his dick to her mouth.

CHAPTER 26: Terry

Terry loved how Maggie didn't even think twice. She just obeyed. He teased the tip of his cock across her bottom lip and she licked it, her tongue hot and wet. He grasped one of the bed posts, the sizzle of her touch shooting from his cock to his balls. He wouldn't be able to do this long. She licked him again and his hips thrust forward, his dick slipping between her lips. She closed around him, sucking and licking.

"Fuck, Maggie." He thrust into her mouth and she gagged. He pulled back but she kept sucking. This time when he thrust, she shifted her head a little and he hit the side of her mouth. It was exquisite. He let go of his dick and clasped her head. "I could come just from this." His balls were already tightening.

She sucked harder, her head bobbing on his cock.

"Fuck me." He pulled back, his dick slipping from her mouth with a pop. He panted, as she stared at him, her mouth red and open, her breasts jiggling with each breath.

He kicked his pants off his ankles before hopping off the bed. He moved behind her. "You are so fucking hot." He said against her ear. "You're my wet dream come true."

"Please, Terry." She wiggled that lush ass against him.

He shoved her skirt up and yanked down her panties. She stepped out of them and he kissed his way down her back, his hands playing with her breasts. He knelt behind her, grabbing her legs and shoving them apart. "You're so wet. You like sucking my cock, don't you?" His fingers trailed down her inner thigh, tracing the moisture that'd escaped her pussy.

"Yes," she gasped as he kissed her leg, tasting her desire for him.

"Lean forward." He nipped her.

She jumped and her legs trembled. "What?"

"The restraints will hold you. Just let yourself fall." He pressed on her lower back and she shifted forward. The position caused her legs to widen, opening herself to him. "So, fucking beautiful." Her pussy was pink and perfect, fragrant and needy for him. He ran one finger through her wetness and she moaned. He couldn't take anymore. "I have to taste you." He buried his face between her legs, kissing and licking along her folds, dragging his tongue up and back, getting closer and closer to her ass hole.

"Terry, stop. What are you doing?"

"Beautiful." He slipped his tongue inside her folds and thrust, fucking her with his mouth.

"Oooh, please...more, Sir. More." She'd flopped forward as far as the restraints allowed, as her lower half pressed backward toward the pleasure.

He slid a finger inside her, flicking her with his tongue. She shook. She was so close, her body tense and waiting to come. He gave her one more long lick and then stood, pulling his finger from her.

"No...please." She stood on her toes, leaning over the bed with her head drooping forward.

"Did I say you could come?"

"I didn't, Sir. But, please. I need to."

"And you will." He positioned himself behind her, rubbing the tip of his cock against her.

"Red." She was looking at him over her shoulder, her breath coming in pants.

"Red?" *Un-fucking believable.* He stopped, his muscles spasming at the betrayal.

"Wait. Yes. Were you with anyone since me?"

He hesitated, not wanting to admit how much he needed her.

"If you were, we have to use a condom."

He sighed. She wasn't going to deny him or herself. He lifted her, pulling her upright and moving so his entire chest was pressed against her back. "There's only been you since the moment I saw you."

Her eyes watered a bit and he kissed her, his hips thrusting slightly against her ass and sliding his dick between those lush cheeks.

"Can we continue?" he asked against her lips.

"Yes, Sir. Please, fuck me, Sir."

CHAPTER 27: Maggie

Maggie jumped as Terry kicked her legs farther apart and then his dick was there, almost where she needed it.

He grabbed her hip, his fingers sinking into her flesh and thrust, the tip of his cock slipping inside her.

"Oh..." She'd forgotten how hot and how big he was.

He rocked his hips, sliding in a little more and she pressed back against him. She needed him inside her all the way. She needed to feel him filling her, hitting those spots that she hadn't known existed until him.

He grabbed her other hip, holding her still as he pushed all the way in. He moaned against her ear. "Fuck, you feel so good."

He pressed against her shoulders, pushing her forward. He grabbed her legs, pulling them up to his hips and she hung, suspended over the foot of the bed. She swayed with his thrusts, sliding over his cock, her breasts bouncing. Her legs tightened around him, trying to center herself, but there was nothing but air and motion, his dick the only solid thing in her world. He pulled almost all the way out and then shoved back inside, filling her and holding her captive for his pleasure.

She moaned, the lack of grounding causing her pussy to clamp around him and making his every move more intense.

"This is what the ponytail is for." He wrapped her hair in his hand, yanking back her head as he continued to thrust into her, harder and faster. "When you wear your hair like this at the Club, you're telling everyone that you want it rough. You want it hard. You want it like this."

He jerked her hair a little harder, the pain on her scalp sending bolts of pleasure to her pussy. His lips came down on her neck, sucking as he fucked her harder and faster. She swayed forward and back, pleasure sparking everywhere—his mouth on her neck, his fingers digging into her hip, the tug of her hair and then his teeth sinking into her neck, nipping her. It was too much. Her body tightened and she screamed, clamping onto his cock as she came, hips shuddering but he held her still, as he rocked into her over and over. He lifted her legs a little and his dick hit a spot that seemed to explode with sensation. She cried out as she spiraled into another orgasm.

His fist tightened in her hair and his thrusts became frenzied, no finesse, no control just lust and need. He grunted against her ear as he came, freezing for one incredible moment before his hips started pumping again, slower now with his release.

His hand moved to her stomach, pulling her up and against him. Her legs dropped to the ground. She wobbled, her bones still liquid, and he steadied her. He unhooked her skirt and shoved it down as he unfastened one hand, wrapping her arm around his neck and then the other. He picked up her limp body and carried her to the bed, crawling in beside her and pulling her close.

"Sleep, sweet rabbit." He kissed her head. "I'm going to need to fuck you again soon."

She kissed the side of his neck. "Good. You owe me some."

CHAPTER 28: Terry

When Terry woke it was still dark. Maggie was draped over him, warm and soft. He could stay like this forever— in bed with her and satiated—but life didn't work that way. He lifted her arm and slipped out from under her leg. He sat up, grabbed his jeans and pulled them on before walking into the living room.

Last night had been fantastic, better than anything he'd ever had. She'd been so open and trusting. He'd fucked her three more times after the first, tying her to the bed, spanking her while his dick was buried inside her. She'd let him do whatever he'd wanted and she'd enjoyed every minute. He couldn't imagine going back to not having her, but she came with a pre-made family.

He sat on the couch next to Beast and scratched the dog's ears. Beast moved so he could lay his large head on Terry's lap.

"What am I going to do, boy?" He stared into the darkness. "I don't want to get used to having kids around and then losing them again." It'd been devastating when it'd happened with his children but at least he'd still been able to see them—not every day, but at least once a week. That wouldn't happen with Maggie's kids. If she left, she'd take her family and he'd be alone. He was used to being alone now. It wasn't so bad, but at first, he'd almost gone crazy—drinking a lot, experimenting with drugs, anything to forget that he'd lost everything that was important to him. He didn't think he'd survive it again.

CHAPTER 29: Maggie

Maggie stretched out her arm, searching for the large, warm, male body, but her hand found nothing but bedding. She sat up, shoving her hair out of her face. Terry's side of the bed was empty.

The bathroom door was open but no light was on. She hopped out of bed, a slight ache between her thighs reminding her of all the wonderful things they'd done last night. She peeked out the window. It was dawn. Saturday. She had no kids and no work. She could stay here all day and make love with Terry.

She stopped at the bathroom door. That's what it was too, at least for her. She had no idea when it'd happened but sometime between when he'd saved her from being raped to when he'd taken care of her and her kids, she'd fallen for him. She shouldn't have. She'd just gotten divorced. Terry should be her rebound lover, but he was far from that.

She went into the bathroom washed her face, brushed her teeth, using his toothbrush, and combed her hair. It was a mess, all tangled and knotty from his hands running through it, tugging on it, making her bend to his will and desires.

When she finished in the bathroom, she was disappointed to see that he still hadn't returned to the bedroom—the bed to be more precise. She'd hoped he would've realized she was awake and would've come to make love again. She hesitated at the door. Her shirt was ruined. She could put on her skirt or underwear but with nothing on top, she felt even more exposed. She grabbed his shirt from the floor, inhaling his scent. A needy ache throbbed between her legs. She was a wanton. Just the thought of him made her want to jump him. She pulled the shirt on over her head and grabbed her underwear before smiling and tossing them aside. He'd be surprised when he realized she'd decided to go commando.

She stepped into the living room and stopped. Terry was on the couch, petting Beast and staring at nothing.

Her stomach fluttered. Something was wrong. "Is everything okay?" She walked toward him. His eyes met hers and her heart stuttered. The look on his face was...She couldn't quite place it—sad, unhappy, haunted. She sat next to him. "Did something happen to someone?"

"Yes. No." He stood, crossing the room. Terry staying away from her wasn't good.

"Tell me what's wrong." As far as she remembered, they'd had a great time last night, but maybe he was regretting it already.

"I'm sorry, Maggie, but I can't. I can't do this."

It felt like every cell in her body died but she stood. "Oh. Okay. I-I guess, I should go."

"Of course, you'll go. That's the problem." He turned

toward her. "That's what I can't handle."

"Terry, I'm not…I can't play games right now." She was barely keeping it together. "Do you want me to leave or not?"

"I don't want you to ever leave," he said softly.

"What?" She took a step toward him, hope flaring in her chest. "What did you say?"

He took a deep breath. "My wife, ex-wife, left me and took our children."

"I thought you saw your kids?"

"I did but I didn't live with them. I didn't see them every night. Tuck them in. Read them stories." His eyes were bright with tears. "Help them with schoolwork. I only got to see them every other weekend and on Tuesdays after school." He ran his hand through his hair. "I hated that. It hurt to lose my wife, my home, my business but it almost killed me to lose my kids."

"I'm sorry." She wanted to hug him and ease the sorrow in this large and powerful man.

"I can't do it again. I can't." He looked up, blinking back tears.

"I don't understand what you're saying." Her feet took a step toward him, unable to stop herself. "I thought you wanted this to be an arrangement—you and me. Nights and weekends without the kids." Her heart was racing, praying he wanted more.

"I did but I can't do that either." He took a step toward her. "I need to see you more. I'm addicted to you. I want to sleep with you at night, every night and wake with you in my arms."

"I have three kids, remember? You don't want to deal with them." She took another step toward him.

"I love kids, especially yours." He took a step and they were now only inches away. "You have no idea how I missed them and you when I came home after you were sick. And then again after you and the kids left here. This place was like a crypt without you—cold, quiet and lifeless."

"Are you saying we should move in together?" This was more than she'd ever hoped.

"I-I don't know." He raised his hand as if to touch her cheek and then dropped his arm. "I don't know what to do. I can't let you move in because I don't know if I'd survive when you left me but I can't stay away from you either."

"Oh, Terry." She bit her lip and smiled.

"It's not funny."

"I know." She reached up and cupped his cheek. "I'm scared too."

"You are?"

"Yes. I'm newly divorced. I'm not supposed to fall in love with the first guy I date."

"You love me?" He looked so nervous and scared, that her heart became a happy pile of mush.

She stood on tiptoe, wrapping her arms around his neck. "Yes. Definitely, yes." She kissed him but he broke away too soon.

"You know, I'm bossy and like to be in control." His hand wandered to her ass. "Not just in the bedroom."

"I know that."

His eyes gleamed as his other hand slipped under the shirt she was wearing. "Naughty girl. You seem to have forgotten your panties."

"Oh, no." She touched her lips. "Does that mean Sir has to punish me?"

He grinned. "Yes, it does." He pulled her against his growing erection.

"I think I need to be punished a lot, Sir."

His smile faded. "First, we need to talk."

"That's a cruel punishment."

He laughed. "Yes, it is, but seriously, you know you're going to have to let me take care of you. It's what I do. What makes me happy."

She dropped down to her feet, her body sliding along his. "I can't."

"You have to."

"I will but not completely."

"Explain." His eyes narrowed and his hand tightened on her ass.

"I'm afraid too and I can't let myself completely rely on anyone anymore. I can't find myself in the position I was in until you helped me with David's lies." She kissed his chin. "I'm working for Annie now. I'm going to make desserts for her business and I'm signing up for classes on baking and business."

"You don't have to do that. You can stay home with the kids. I have enough money—"

"This isn't about your money or my money. This is about me being able to survive on my own."

"But you don't have to be on your own, ever."

"I love you, Terry, but I have to do this for me. Please try and understand." She touched his cheek. "This has nothing to do with me not trusting you. I want to know that I'm with you because I want to be and not because I need to be. I want, no need, to be able to support myself, just in case."

"Maggie, please don't do this." He rested his chin on the

top of her head. "Let me take care of you."

"You can." She put her cheek on his chest. "You can listen to me when I come home. Taste my desserts. Help me with the kids. You can massage my feet after a long day and you can take care of me by being in my life."

"What if that's not enough?"

"It will be." She looked up at him and he was terrified. "Terry, I don't stop loving people. They stop loving me."

"Me too." He skimmed his thumb over her cheek.

"Then, I think we'll be stuck with each other forever."

"I hope so."

"Me too." She pressed against him a little more, feeling his growing need.

"However…" He grinned.

"Yes." She knew that gleam in his eyes. He was going to be naughty again and she couldn't wait.

"I will need you to make some clit cakes or titty treats. It's a deal breaker if you don't, because I intend to feast on your body every night for the rest of my life."

Her face heated. "Actually, I already did some research on that."

"You did?"

"Yep. I should have something for you to try soon."

"How about this weekend?" He lifted her by her ass. "We'll go to the store later and get all the ingredients. Honey. We definitely need honey."

She wrapped her arms around his neck. "You got it and I think we'll put some on you too." She smiled against his lips. "I love honey."

Hope you enjoyed His Mission.

See below for a sneak peek of Interviewing for her Lover (Nick and Sarah's story) and The Voyeur (Patrick and Annie's story). They're both free on all ebook retailers. You can get the entire Six Nights of Sins series (Nick and Sarah's six nights of kinky fun) for free. A thank you gift for joining my newsletter.

Here's What You Get When You
Join My Readers' Group

Win Before You Can Buy
Exclusive Giveaways
Free Books
Sneak Peeks

Go to my website or email me for details:

https://www.EllisODay.com

authorellisoday@gmail.com

Interviewing For Her Lover

CHAPTER 1: SARAH

"Do I have to take off my clothes?" Sarah tugged on the hem of her black dress. It was shorter and lower cut in the front than she normally wore, but the Viewing was about finding a man for sex and according to Ethan men liked to look.

"No." Ethan turned her away from the door and forced her to look at him. "You don't have to do anything you don't want to do."

She stared into his blue eyes. Why couldn't he be interested in her? She'd only met with him five or six times, but she trusted him. He ran his business, La Petite Mort Club, very professionally and he was gorgeous with his sandy brown hair, strong cheekbones and vibrant blue eyes. Sex between them would be good. Easy. He was attractive and...not for her. She didn't want decent sex or good sex, she wanted mind blowing, screaming orgasms and that wouldn't happen between him and her because there was no chemistry, no attraction.

"Listen to me." He moved his hands to her shoulders and gave her a gentle shake. "You aren't selling yourself to the highest bidder. You're looking for a partner. One who'll"—he grinned—"turn you on in ways you can't even imagine."

She glanced at the door where the men waited. Waited for her. Waited to decide if they wanted to fuck her. "I'm a bit nervous."

"About what?"

This was embarrassing but she'd been honest with him up to this point. She'd had to be. He was helping her...had helped her to choose the five men in the other room. "What if none of them..."

"They will want you." He touched her chin, turning her face toward him. "A few of them may back out after this but not because they don't want you."

"Yeah, right."

"I'm only going to say this once. You're beautiful and different, unique."

"That's not necessarily a good thing." She had long legs and a nice body—trim and firm—but with her auburn hair and green eyes she was cute at best, not gorgeous. The men she'd chosen were all rich, good looking and powerful. They could have anyone they wanted.

"It's exactly what they want, or most of them anyway." He took her hand and led her closer to the door.

She leaned on his arm, hating these shoes. She should've stuck with her flats but Ethan had given her a list of what she should wear and high heels were on the top. She'd found the smallest heels in the store and by Ethan's look when he'd first seen her she might've been better off going barefoot. He'd met her at the private entrance and his gaze had been appreciating as it'd skimmed over her dress, until he got to her feet. Then he'd frowned and shook his head.

"Finding the right men for you wasn't easy." He stopped at the door.

"Thanks a lot." She shifted away from him, his words hurting a little. She hadn't been sure of her appeal to the opposite sex in a long time, not since the early years with Adam.

"It's not because you aren't beautiful but because you want to be dominated and you want to dominate—"

"I do not want to dominate." All she could picture was a woman in black leather with a whip and that wasn't her, not at all.

"If you say so." He smiled a little. "But, you do want to lead the scene. Right? Because that's what—"

"Yes." Her face was red. She could feel it. She didn't want to talk about her fantasies again. It'd been embarrassing enough the first time, but he'd had to know what she wanted to compile a list of candidates.

"Most at the club are either doms or subs. Very few are switches." His eyes raked over her. "That's what's so special about you. You want it all and…that's what made choosing these men difficult."

He'd given her a selection of twenty-two men who

might be interested in what she wanted. She'd narrowed it down to seven. Two had been uninterested when he'd approached. That'd left her with the five who'd see her in person for the first time tonight, but she wouldn't see them. That'd come after the Viewing when she interviewed any who were still interested.

"Remember what you want. This is your deal. You call the shots. At least a little." He kissed her forehead. "But don't refuse to give them anything. You don't want a submissive."

"No." That didn't turn her on at all and she only had eight weeks. One night each week for two months before she'd go back to her lonely life, her lonely bed, dreaming of Adam.

"You can do this." He pulled a flask from his jacket and unscrewed the lid. "For courage."

"Thanks." She took a large swallow, the brandy too thick and sweet for her taste but it was better than nothing.

"Now, go find your lover."

She laughed a little but sadness swept through her. There'd be no love between this man and herself. This would be sex, fucking. That's all. The only man she'd ever love, her only lover, was dead. This was purely physical. "Thank you again." She stood on tip-toe and kissed his cheek. He may be gorgeous and run a sex club but he was a good man, a good friend.

She turned and opened the door and walked into the room, trying to stay balanced on these stupid heels. Men wouldn't find them so attractive if they had to wear them. The room was dark except for one light highlighting a small platform. That was for her. She stepped up onto the small stage. The room was silent but they were there, above her, hidden behind the one-way mirrors, watching and deciding if they wanted to take the next step—to eventually take her.

She stared into the blackness of the room. It wasn't huge but its emptiness made it seem vast. She glanced upward, the light making her squint and she quickly stared back into the darkness. This was arranged for them to see her. That was it. She'd get no glimpse of them yet. She'd seen their pictures, chosen them but meeting them in person would be different. A picture couldn't tell her their smell or the sound of their voices.

She tugged at her dress where it hugged her hips, wishing the questions would start, but there was only silence. She shifted, the heels already killing her feet. Ethan hadn't liked them and if they weren't going to impress, she might as well take them off. She moved to the back of the stage, leaned against the wall and removed her shoes. As she returned to the center of the stage a man spoke, his voice loud and commanding almost echoing throughout the room.

"Don't stop there. Take off your dress."

She bent, placing her shoes on the floor. That wasn't part of the deal. She wasn't going to undress in front of five men, only one. Only the one she chose. She straightened. "No."

"What?" He was surprised and not happy.

"I said no. That's not part of the Viewing."

"I want to see what I'm getting."

She stared up toward the windows, squinting a little. She couldn't tell from where the voice had come. The speaker system made it sound as if it were coming from God himself. "And you will if I pick you."

Another man laughed.

"It's not funny. She's disobedient," said the man with the loud voice.

"Not always. I can be obedient." These men liked to be in control but sometimes, so did she.

"Will you raise your dress? Just a little," asked another voice.

"Didn't you see enough in the photos?" She'd applied

a few months ago for this one-time contract. She'd been excited and nervous when she'd received the acceptance email with an appointment for a photography session. She'd never had her picture professionally taken, since she didn't count school portraits or the ones her parents had had done at JCPenny's. She'd been anxious and a little turned on imaging wearing her new lingerie in front of a strange man, so she'd been disappointed to find the photographer was an elderly woman, but the lady had put her at ease and the photos had turned out better than she'd expected. She glanced up at the mirrors, hoping she wasn't disappointing all the men. That'd be too embarrassing.

"Those were...nice, but I'd like to see the real thing before deciding if you're worth my time."

She raised a brow. "You can always leave." She shouldn't antagonize him. She was sure the bossy man had already decided against committing to this agreement. Disobedience didn't appeal to him. That left four. If she didn't pick any of them, she could go through the process again, but she didn't think she would.

The man chuckled slightly. "I know that, but I haven't decided I don't want to fuck you. Not yet, anyway."

The word, so harsh and vulgar excited her. It was the truth. That was what she, what they were all deciding.

Who'd get to fuck her. It was what she wanted, what she'd agreed to do, and as much as she dreaded it, she wanted it. She was tired of being alone. She missed having a man inside her—his tongue and fingers and cock.

"Do any of you have any questions?" She clasped her dress at her waist and slowly gathered it upward, displaying more and more of her long legs. She ran. They were in shape. The men would like them.

"Lower your top," said the same man who'd told her to take off her dress.

She didn't like him. If he didn't back out, she'd have Ethan remove him from her list. He was too commanding. He'd never allow her to be in control.

"I don't know if he's done looking at my legs yet." She continued raising the dress until her black and green lace panties were almost exposed.

"Very nice and thank you," said the polite man.

"You're welcome." This man might work. She shifted the dress up another inch before dropping it, giving them a glance at her panties.

"Now, your top," said the bossy guy.

She lowered her spaghetti string off one shoulder, letting the dress dip, but not enough to show anything besides the side of her bra.

"More," he said.

"No." She raised the strap, covering herself. She didn't like this man and wished he'd leave. She'd kick him out but that wasn't part of the process and they were very firm about their rules at this club.

"He got to see your pussy. Why don't I get to see your tits?"

"You got to see as much as he did." She was ready to move on. She bent and picked up her shoes. "If there's nothing else, gentleman, we can set up times for the interview process."

"Turn around," said another man.

It was a command, but she didn't mind. There was a politeness to his order and something about the texture of his voice caused an ache between her thighs. There was a caress in his tone but with an edge and a promise of a good hard fuck.

"Are you going to obey?" His words were whisper soft and smooth.

"Yes." That was going to be part of this too. Her commanding and him commanding. She dropped her shoes and turned.

"Raise you dress again."

She looked over her shoulder at where she imagined he

sat watching her.

"Please." There was humor in his tone.

She smiled and slowly gathered the dress upward. She stopped right below the curve of her bottom.

"More. Please." There was a little less humor in his voice.

She wanted to show him her ass. She wanted to show that voice everything but not with the others around. This would be just her and one man, one stranger. That was one of her rules. "No. Only if you're picked do you get to see any more of me than you have." She dropped her dress, grabbed her shoes and walked off the stage and out the door.

She was going to have sex with a stranger. She was going to live out her fantasies for eight nights with a man she didn't know and would never really know, but she wasn't going to lose who she was. She'd keep her honor and her dignity which meant she had to pick a man who'd agree with her rules.

Get your free ebook copy.

http://books2read.com/u/3nYKo6

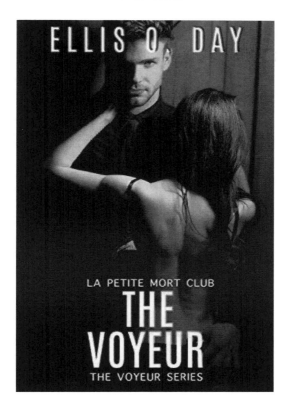

The Voyeur

CHAPTER 1: ANNIE

Annie finished making the bed and gathered the sheets from the floor, keeping them as far away from her body as possible. These sex rooms were disgusting and Ethan was a jerk making her work as a maid. She almost had her Bachelor's Degree in Culinary Arts, but he'd refused to hire her for the kitchen—too many men in the kitchen. The only job he'd give her at La Petite Mort Club was as a maid and unfortunately, she needed the money too badly to refuse.

She stuffed the dirty sheets into the cart and hurried out the door. She had almost thirty minutes before she had to be at the next "sex room." She hid the cart in a closet and darted down a back hallway, staying clear of the cameras. Julie, the woman who supervised the daytime maids, was a real bitch. If she were caught sneaking away from her duties, she'd be assigned to the orgy rooms every day. Right now, they all took turns cleaning that nightmare. She swore they should get hazard pay to even go in those rooms.

She slipped through a doorway and hurried to the one-way mirror. She stared at the couple in the next room. From her first day here, she'd been curious about the activities at the club. She was twenty-four and wasn't a virgin but she'd never, ever done some of these things.

The woman in the room below was tied to a table, legs spread and wearing some sort of leather outfit that left her large breasts free and her crotch exposed. She had shaved her pussy and her pink lower lips were swollen and glistening from her excitement. The man strolled around the table as if he had all night. He still had his pants on but had removed his shirt. His arms and chest were well defined but he had a slight paunch. His erection tented his pants and Annie felt wetness pool between her legs. She had no idea why watching this turned her on but it did.

Ever since she'd accidentally barged in on that guy and girl in the Interview room, she couldn't stop watching.

The man below ran his hand up the woman's inner thigh, glancing over her pussy. The woman thrust her hips upward and Annie ran her own hand between her legs. The man's mouth moved but Annie couldn't hear anything and then he slapped the woman across the thigh hard enough to leave a red mark. Annie jumped. She wasn't into that, but she couldn't stop watching the woman's face. At first, it'd contorted in pain but then it'd morphed into pleasure. The man hit her again and then bent, kissing the red welts— running his tongue across them as his fingers squeezed her nipple.

Annie clutched her thighs together, searching for some relief. Her panties were soaked. It wouldn't take but a few strokes to make her come. She started to slide her hand into her pants.

"Having fun?" asked a deep voice from behind her.

She spun around, her heart dropping into her stomach. "Ah…I was just finishing cleaning in here." Damn, she should've closed the door but she hadn't expected anyone in this area. The rooms were off limits on this floor until tonight and she was the only one assigned to clean here.

He shut the door and locked it before strolling toward her. She'd seen him around the Club, but more than that she remembered him from the military photos her brother, Vic, had sent to her. She carried one of the three of them—Vic, Ethan and this guy, Patrick—in her purse. He'd been attractive in the picture, but now that he was older and in person he was gorgeous. He had dark green eyes, brown hair and a perfect body. He stopped so close to her his chest almost brushed against her breasts. She was pretty sure it would if she inhaled deeply. She really wanted to take that deep breath and feel his hard chest against her breasts.

"Don't let me stop you from enjoying the show."

"I…I wasn't. I should go." She started to walk past him but he grabbed her hand.

His grip was warm and strong but loose enough that she could pull free if she wanted. She didn't. Even though she only knew him from her brother's pictures and letters, she'd had many fantasies about him when she'd been in high school. Her gaze dropped to the front of his pants and her mouth almost watered. He was definitely interested. She dragged her eyes up his body, stopping on his face. He smiled at her.

"There's nothing to be embarrassed about. Watching turns us all on." He kissed the back of her hand and she jumped as his tongue darted out, tasting her skin.

"I…I should go." She didn't move.

"No, you should watch." He dropped her hand and grabbed her shoulders, gently turning her toward the mirror. He trailed his hands up and down her arms. "Watch."

The man in the other room was now sucking on the woman's breast as his fingers caressed her pussy.

"Would you like to hear them? Or do you like it quiet?" His voice was a rough whisper against her ear.

"Sound, please." She wanted to hear their gasps and moans. She wanted to close her eyes and pretend it was her. She shifted, squeezing her thighs together.

He chuckled as he moved away. She felt his absence to her bones. He'd been strong and warm behind her and for a moment she'd felt safe, safer than she had since her brother had come back from the war, broken and sad, and her father had started drinking again.

The woman's moans filled the room and Patrick came back to stand behind her, this time placing his hands on her waist.

"I'm Patrick," he said against her ear.

She couldn't take her eyes from the scene in front of her. The woman was almost coming as the man thrust his fingers inside of her.

"What's your name?" He nipped her neck and she jumped.

"I...I..." If she told him her name, he might say something to Ethan. Ethan would kill her if he knew she was in here watching.

"Tell me your name." His lips trailed along her neck and she tipped her head giving him better access.

The guy was kissing his way down the woman's body. Annie wanted to touch herself, to make herself come but Patrick was here.

He nibbled her ear. "Why won't you tell me your name?"

"I...I'll get in trouble." She rubbed her ass against his erection, hopefully giving him a hint.

"Tease." His hand drifted down her stomach, stopping right above where she wanted him to touch. "Tell me your name or I'll make you suffer." He unbuttoned her pants and left his hand—warm, rough but immobile—resting on her abdomen.

"I can't." She stood on tip-toe, hoping his hand would lower a little but he was too tall or she was too short. He had to be almost six foot and she was barely five-foot four. "I could get fired and I need this job."

"Darling, Ethan won't fire you for fucking a customer."

"We can't." She spun around. She hadn't thought this through. He was her fantasy come to life and she wanted him to be hers just for a moment, but Ethan would find out and then she'd be in deep shit.

"Don't worry. I'm a member and you work here, so we're both clean." He hesitated, his hands tightening on her hips. "Are you protected?"

"What?" She had no idea what he was talking about.

"Ethan makes sure everyone at the Club is clean but only the...some of his employees are required to be on birth control." He ran his hands up her sides, getting closer and closer to her breasts. "Are you on birth control?" His eyes darkened as they dropped to her tits. "If not, it's okay. There are other things we can do."

Oh, she wanted to do everything his eyes promised, but she couldn't. "No, I'll get in trouble. I need this job. I have to go." She tried to move but her feet refused to obey, so she just stared at his handsome face.

"Are you sure?" He bent so he was almost eye level with her. "I promise. Ethan won't care. A lot of maids become...change jobs. The pay's a lot better." His eyes roamed over her frame. "Especially, for someone as cute as you."

Ethan would kill her before letting her become one of his pleasure associates.

"I could talk to Ethan for you." His hands moved up her body, stopping right below her breasts.

Her nipples hardened and she forgot everything but what he was making her feel. He ran his thumb over one of them and she leaned closer, wanting him to do it again.

He did. He continued rubbing her nipple as he spoke. "I could persuade him to let me...handle your initiation into club life."

Her heart raced in her chest. It could be just her and him doing all these things she'd seen. Her pussy throbbed but she couldn't do it. She wouldn't do it. She couldn't have sex for money. Her parents were both dead but they'd never understand and she couldn't disappoint them. "No. I can't do that...not for money." Her eyes darted to the door. She needed to get out of there before she did something she'd regret.

"That's even better." He smiled as he stepped closer. "We can keep this between us. No money. Only a man and a woman." He leaned down and whispered in her ear, "Giving each other pleasure. A lot of pleasure. In ways you haven't even imagined."

There were moans from the other room and she glanced over her shoulder. The man's face was buried between the woman's thighs.

Patrick turned her around, pulling her against him and wrapping his arms around her waist. "Are you wet?"

"What? No." She struggled in his arms, her ass brushing against his erection again.

"Oh fuck. Do that again." He kissed her neck, open mouthed and hot.

She stopped trying to get away. She wanted this…this moment. She shouldn't but she did, so she wiggled her butt against him again. He was hard and long and her body ached for him. It'd been too long since she'd had sex. She needed this.

"Would you like me to touch you?" His hands drifted over her hips and down her thighs.

She'd like him to do all sorts of things to her. She nodded.

"Say it." His words were a command she couldn't disobey.

"Yes."

"Yes, what?" He untucked her shirt from her pants.

"Touch me. Please." She was already pushing her hips toward his hand. She wanted his hand on her, his fingers inside of her.

"Are you wet?" he asked again.

She inhaled sharply as he unzipped her pants.

"Don't lie to me. I'll find out in a minute."

She'd never talked dirty during sex and she wasn't sure she was ready to do that with a stranger. Her heart skipped a beat. Maybe, she shouldn't be doing any of this with a stranger. She grabbed his hand. "Maybe, we shouldn't."

The woman below cried out and the man straightened, wiping his face and unbuttoning his pants.

"Watch. The main event is about to happen." Patrick's hot breath tickled her neck.

Her gaze locked on the man's penis. It was large and demanding. He straddled the woman, grabbing his cock.

"Don't you want to feel some of what they feel?" He nibbled on her ear and then neck. "I can help you."

She may not know him, but she trusted him. He was a former marine. He'd been a good friend of Vic's. He wouldn't hurt her and she needed to come. She loosened her grip, letting go of his hand. He slipped inside her pants, caressing her pussy through her underwear. His fingers were long and strong. She closed her eyes, leaning against him as he stroked her.

"You're already so wet and hot." His breath was a warm caress on her ear. "But, I'm going to make you wetter and then, I'm going to make you come." His other hand shoved her pants down, giving him more room to work. "Open your eyes and watch the show."

She did as he said. The man was inside the woman, thrusting hard and fast. The woman was moaning and trying to move but the restraints kept her mostly helpless.

"Fuck, you're soaked." Patrick's hand cupped her and she arched into his touch, rubbing her ass against his erection. He shoved his hand inside her underwear, his finger running along her folds until he slipped one inside.

"Oh." She grabbed his hand—not to push him away, but to make sure he didn't leave.

He smiled against her hair. "Don't worry, baby. I won't stop." He stroked his finger inside of her and his wrist brushed against her clit.

She needed more. She needed to touch him, feel him. She turned her head, wrapping her arms up and around his neck. He kissed her. It was desperate and wild, but he stopped too soon.

"They're almost done. You don't want to miss it."

She turned back to the mirror. The man below continued to fuck the woman as Patrick finger-fucked her. His other hand slipped under her shirt to her breast. His lips sucked her neck as he rocked his erection against her ass. He was everywhere, and she was so close. The muscles in her legs constricted. Her hips tipped upward.

"Wait, baby," he groaned in her ear, as he pushed a second finger inside of her. "Just a few more minutes."

His fingers were stretching her and it felt wonderful. She moaned, long and low as he thrust harder and faster, almost matching the pace of the man in the other room. She could almost imagine it was Patrick's cock and not his fingers inside of her.

"Oh…oh," she cried out. He was pushing her toward the edge. Her body was spiraling with each pump of his fingers. She was going to come—right here while watching that couple. It was so dirty and so wrong and it only made her hotter.

The woman below screamed and her body stiffened. The man thrust again and again and then grunted his release.

"Show's over." Patrick nipped her neck at the same time he pressed down on her clit with his thumb, sending her shooting into her orgasm.

She trembled and he pulled her close, his hand still cupping her pussy and his fingers still inside of her. When her heartbeat had settled, he removed his hand and bent, pulling off her shoes and removing her pants before lifting her and carrying her to the wall.

"My turn." He wrapped her legs around his waist.

Her phone rang. "My work phone. I…I have to answer it."

"When we're done." He unzipped his pants.

"Annie, answer the phone. I know you're around here. I can hear it ringing you stupid bitch," yelled Julie.

"Oh, shit." She shoved Patrick away, and ran across the room, grabbing her clothes off the floor. "It's my boss. She'll kill me if she finds me like this."

"I'll take care of Julie." He headed for the door, zipping up his fly. "Don't move." He grinned over his shoulder at her. "You can take off your pants again, but other than that, don't move."

"No. Please." She raced over to him, grabbing his arm. "I need this job." And Ethan could not find out about this.

"She won't fire you. She can't. Only Ethan can fire you." He bent and kissed her.

His lips were gentle and coaxing this time and her body swayed into him. He pulled her even closer and she could feel his cock, thick and heavy, pushing against her. Her pussy tightened again in anticipation.

"Damnit, Annie. This is going to be so much worse if I have to call your stupid phone again. Get out here!" Julie was only a few doors down.

She grabbed Patrick and tugged on his hand. "Please, hide." She glanced around, looking for somewhere that would conceal a six-foot muscular man.

"I'm not going to hide from Julie."

Get your free ebook and find out what happens next.
http://books2read.com/u/38r9Ka

Coming soon:

GO TO MY WEBSITE TO SEE ALL MY BOOKS AND TO SEE WHAT'S COMING NEXT
HTTPS://WWW.ELLISODAY.COM

ETHAN'S STORY
MATTIE'S STORY
A LA PETITE MORT CLUB CHRISTMAS
JAKE'S STORY
HUNTER'S STORY
DESIREE'S STORY

Email me with questions, concerns or to let me know what you thought of the book. I love hearing from readers.
authorellisoday@gmail.com

Follow me.
Facebook
https://www.facebook.com/EllisODayRom anceAuthor/

Twitter
https://twitter.com/ellis_o_day

Pinterest
www.pinterest.com\AuthorEllisODay

ABOUT THE AUTHOR

Ellis O. Day loves reading and writing about love and sex. She believes that although the two don't have to go together, it's best when they do (both in life and in fantasy).

Printed in Great Britain
by Amazon

20940724R00082